Kinder County: Sins & Secrets

By R. M. Shiver

To my beloved Jocko.

One of the greatest detectives of his generation.

Table of Contents

Part I

The two sisters were both school teachers who had recently graduated from a Teacher's College in the nation's capital. They were eager to begin work, and willing to go anywhere in the country to teach, as long as they could remain together and teach at the same school. This was during a period of time when country schools were located in remote, undeveloped areas, and many schools were designated as one-room schools. One-room schools consisted of one large open room where often students in grades 1 through 10 or 11 interacted together under the tutelage sometimes of only one teacher. The teacher or teachers, if there happened to be more than one, assigned to such schools had to be skilled and adept enough to teach all levels of students in all grades under one roof.

It just so happened that there was a one-room school in coastal, southeastern Xenolina that needed two teachers, where the school superintendent of Kinder County had contacted the State Board of Education seeking two qualified teachers to manage a school of approximately 25 students ages 6 through 17 in classes ranging from grades 1 through 11. The Xenolina State Board of Education had shared the request, as was customary, with the Federal Office of Education in

Washington, D.C. Fortunately, in this case, two young teachers, Marie and Madesyn Moore, had recently applied for any available teaching positions, and their applications were pulled for perusal. On the surface, it appeared that they would be a perfect fit to fill the positions, so the Federal Office of Education staff contacted the sisters and requested that they come downtown for an interview. For Marie and Madesyn--who had been anxious and apprehensive about finding employment after having just completed four years of education that included practice teaching--receiving the call from the Office of Education was a godsend. Their excitement reverberated throughout their parents' home as they hugged, danced, and exclaimed their good fortune. The only drawback, it seemed, was if accepted for the positions, the sisters would be teaching in an area that was approximately 400 miles from their home in Washington, D.C. This fact, while unpleasant for their parents, heightened the girls' excitement because it would validate the idea of the new-found independence they had been pining for during their last year in college.

When the day of the interviews finally arrived, the interviewers questioned the two young ladies as a team, since the job arrangement required teamwork between the two individuals who would be fortunate enough to land the jobs. Both Marie and Madesyn were charismatic, smart, intelligent, witty, compassionate, and industrious. During their years of studies, both had been honor students who remained on the Dean's List their entire four years at the Teachers' College. After having reviewed their credentials, and during the interview, the interviewers made a foregone conclusion that if these two ladies were willing to accept the employment that was being offered, the jobs were theirs. Marie and Madesyn were told shortly after the interview terminated that within a period of 10 days they would be notified of the board's decision as to whether or not they would be going south as newly employed school teachers.

Because it was June already, if given the jobs, the two sisters would only have approximately six weeks to tie up loose ends in the city, go south and find a place to live—hopefully in close proximity to the school as neither of them owned an automobile and public transportation was a foreign concept in rural areas of the south—come back to D.C. and pack, then make the trek back to Xenolina. Somehow, they managed to get everything done in record time. And by this time their excitement had escalated to an even higher level. With all tasks completed, Marie and Madesyn bid their parents farewell on a beautiful summer day, and set out to begin a new life. On the evening of July 15, Marie and Madesyn boarded the train in Washington, D.C., and prepared for the all-night ride that would take them to their destination of the Kinder County town of Granite Point, community of Hawk Town, in the State of Xenolina. If all went as scheduled, they would arrive in the early morning hours of July 16. A truck would be waiting at the train depot to take them and all their belongings to their new home near the school to which they had been assigned.

The long ride on the train was relaxing. Both sisters had reading materials to prevent them from getting bored when they were not sleeping or engaged in conversation. For the most part, the trip was quite pleasant. The sisters enjoyed a late supper in the dining car, where they became enraptured in conversation with other travelers. Once they returned to their assigned seats, it wasn't long before they fell asleep and slept until morning. By the time they reached their destination, they were anxious to gather their belongings and head straight away to their new home.

In their search for a place to live, they had found a lovely two-story cottage located within walking distance of the school and close to the Northeast Cape Dread

River. It was located in the nice community of Hawk Town, offering comfortable living standards of the 1940s. The cottage was white, although it had been a number of years since it had been freshly painted. But while the paint had faded, the cottage by no means appeared to be unkempt. There were rambling roses climbing trellises on either side of the yard, and evergreen shrubbery at all four corners of the house. Two large pecan trees stood in the backyard, inviting visitors to sit and chill out in the shade. A chinaberry tree graced the western side yard. Plum bushes were interspersed in a nearby hedge row. An apple tree and a pear tree had stationed themselves away from the house on the eastern side of the yard. The teachers would have homegrown fresh fruits and nuts to supplement their diets in wholesome fashion.

Inside the cottage itself, someone, a few years back, had papered the walls in every room except the kitchen, which had been recently painted a soft chartreuse. The kitchen was the large eat-in type containing an oak table with seating for eight. A butcher's block was located in a corner near the pantry. The cast-iron stove sported a reservoir next to the oven, with double warming bins overhead. There were more wall cabinets than Marie and Madesyn needed for food and dish storage, so they had decided to use some of the cabinets to store books and teaching supplies. The large kitchen made a perfect setting as a dual kitchen-office. In the adjoining living room, there was a divan, two wingback chairs upholstered in crushed blue velvet, two mahogany end tables, lamps, and a matching mahogany coffee table. There were no paintings on the walls and no curtains at the windows. But Marie and Madesyn would soon take care of that housekeeping/decorating tidbit. The stairway led upstairs to two reasonably-sized bedrooms and one smaller room that would be used as the chamber room. The cottage was absolutely perfect as far as Marie and Madesyn were concerned.

Upon arrival at the Granite Point Depot in Kinder County, Xenolina, the sisters were met by a polite and handsome young man named Teddy Stapleton, who informed them that the Kinder County School Superintendent had hired his father to transport them from the depot to their cottage. But, Teddy explained, his father was not feeling well this morning and had asked him to fetch the ladies and take them to their new home. He then loaded their luggage and boxes on the back of the truck and the three of them squeezed inside the truck's cab. Along the route, Teddy pointed out landmarks of interest, family farms, the general store, post office, and of course, the school. Teddy informed Marie and Madesyn that he had their keys to the school building, and asked if any of the boxes needed to be dropped off at the school. Some of the boxes did have items to be taken to the school, so it was a great idea to leave those boxes now because it would be less hassle than having to take the boxes home, and bring them back to the school later.

Excitedly, Marie and Madesyn asked Teddy to stop at the school, making their first official stop in their new community. When they unlocked the door and entered the building, they were met by a musky smell because the building had been shut since school had closed two months earlier in May for summer vacation. Marie and Madesyn got a sense of the magnitude of the job that would be necessary to get the open-space, one-room school ready to receive students in August. They had only three weeks to get the job done before the first day of school for students, which was August 6.

Teddy, being both observant and sensitive, discerned the anticipated chores facing the two school teachers. He asked if he could help them in their preparation for the first day of school by helping them with the heavy cleaning job confronting them. Marie and Madesyn felt a great sense of relief at Teddy's offer, and gladly accepted. After all school supplies had been unloaded, the trio set out for the cottage. At the cottage, they unloaded everything remaining in the truck and offered Teddy a tip for being so helpful in a gentlemanly way. He refused, of course, and promised to return the next morning at 8 a.m.

After Teddy's departure, the very first task the sisters tackled was opening all of the windows. Marie began downstairs while Madesyn dashed upstairs to complete the job. Although the outside temperature was hot, there was a breeze blowing due to an impending summer storm. There were frequent thunder storms in Granite Point during the hot summer months. Marie reminded Madesyn that once the rain began to fall, they would have to close all the windows again. But, in the meantime, the fresh air coming through the open windows was most inviting.

**

By the time Teddy returned home, his father, Clemis, was up and stirring about. He asked Teddy, "Did you do a good job for me, son? And take care of the ladies alright?" Teddy assured his dad that everything had been taken care of, and the two young school teachers were settling into what would be their home for the next several years. Marie and Madesyn had signed a two-year contract with the Kinder County superintendent of schools. Clemis stated that he was beginning to feel better, so perhaps later in the day he would drive over and introduce himself to the young ladies.

In the meantime, there were 11 hungry children waiting for breakfast. The eldest girl, Cora, had already made two pans of biscuits and was busy frying bacon, ham, and sausage. In a few minutes, after the meats were ready, she would scramble two dozen eggs. Fortunately for the Stapleton family, all of their hens were still laying eggs. Clemis often wondered how he had been able to manage such a large family after his wife, Dorothy, had died giving birth to their youngest child, Peggy. He also wondered whether or not he would be able to court and eventually marry again. Wooing a woman was difficult—damned near impossible—when there were 11 children in the picture. What woman in these hard times wanted a ready-made family? A huge one that consisted of a husband and 11 children! Clemis had never been hopeful and had resigned himself to being a widower for the rest of his natural life, even though he was only 39 years old. But sometimes he did dream of having a beautiful, loving wife who would be a good mother to his 11 children.

After all the Stapleton family had finished breakfast, the older kids got busy with their daily chores—picking beans, chopping wood, as the old wood-burning stove provided the only means of cooking, washing clothes (a daily chore because each child had very few decent items of clothing to wear), milking the cows, and trimming bushes and chopping grass, since vegetation grew extremely fast during the summer. Even though it was still morning, Clemis thought, "Why wait until the afternoon?" While the kids are busy, this would be an ideal time for him to pay the new school teachers a visit.

Marie and Madesyn were surprised to see the old truck chugging up the road because Teddy had only been gone approximately two or three hours, and he had promised to return the next day. But as the old truck drew nearer to the house, they could see that Teddy was not the man behind the wheel.

As Clemis exited the truck wearing a big bright smile, the two sisters stepped off the porch and waited for Clemis to introduce himself and state his business. "How do you ladies do?" Clemis asked. "My name is

Clemis Stapleton and the young man who assisted you this morning is my son."

"What a fine young man he is," Madesyn replied. And Marie chimed in her agreement.

"Thank you both, kindly," was Clemis' reply. He said he had just stopped by to see if they needed anything else with which he could help. Both ladies expressed their appreciation, but assured Clemis that for the time being, they were managing fine with unpacking and putting things in place.

Madesyn offered Clemis a glass of iced tea, which he eagerly accepted. Since she and Marie were at the point of taking a break anyway, they sat on the porch with Clemis and enjoyed a cold glass of iced tea as well. But after what seemed to be a bit too long for a first-time visit, Marie told Clemis that she and Madesyn needed to get back to their unpacking and putting the house in order. Although Clemis seemed reluctant to get the message, he finally thanked them for the tea and left.

Marie told Madesyn that she couldn't quite put her finger on it, but there was something about Clemis that made her feel a bit uneasy. Madesyn laughed and told her sister that her kismet was going haywire. She added that Clemis was simply displaying the social skills of a local yokel.

A few days later, Clemis seemed distant, as if he were daydreaming and out of touch with the daily routine demands of his large family. Teddy noticed the change in his father's demeanor but although he was a bit concerned, he did not feel he could broach the subject of Clemis' seemingly sudden lack of interest in routine family matters.

***

On Wednesday evenings it was customary for the ladies of the Hawk Town community to participate in Bible Study while the men of the community gathered at a joint called Buster's Place. Buster was a community icon—single, had been away to war, and was known for his numerous stories of himself as a war hero. He had the reputation of being one of the best bootleggers in the region, second only to Clemis, who happened to be Buster's supplier. So, there was always a lot of activity at Buster's Place, not just on the weekends, but on Wednesday nights as well. People came from far and near to purchase or sample Buster's good wine. And, of course, the local men had established Buster's Place as their Wednesday night hangout.

One Wednesday night a few weeks following Clemis' visit with Marie and Madesyn, Clemis' ego was in bloom when he joined the boys at Buster's Place. Clemis had suddenly switched from being one who talked incessantly about his children, to a man who seemed to have become enamored with one of the new school teachers who had recently come to the community. When it appeared that the guys weren't taking Clemis seriously as he exaggerated imaginable details of the extent of his first and only visit with the young school teachers, Clemis got angry. The men began to laugh at his blather and Clemis reacted by drinking until he became sozzled. The last notion Clemis tried to impress upon his pals before he headed home was that one day he was going to marry one of those school teachers.

In the days that followed, Clemis began to devise a plan to woo Marie and Madesyn. The first action he planned was to go to the school house daily near the end of the school day and begin making some unnecessary repairs. He was going to begin by shoring up the steps to the old building. He hoped that the teachers would notice how accommodating he was, and would perhaps invite him to dinner one evening.

As days passed, Marie and Madesyn could not help but notice Clemis and his handy man actions around the school. Both ladies expressed their gratitude to Clemis for being a terrific parent and tremendous supporter of the school. Clemis mistook their compliments of his work as a special affection toward him. By this time, he had decided that it was Madesyn, the younger sister, whom he was going to one day marry. It seemed to Clemis that of the two women, Madesyn was more suitable to be the mother of his children, because his baby girl, Peggy, simply adored Madesyn and would pine for her in the evenings after school, and sometimes during the night.

***

On a subsequent Wednesday night visit to Buster's Place, Clemis was guarded in his speech after having been so open, excited, and braggart about his impending pursuit of the school teachers. He vowed not to share his feelings about the teachers, especially Madesyn, anymore with the guys he hung out with at Buster's Place until he knew he had Madesyn's undivided attention and affection. He felt that it would be a colossal mistake to say more at this juncture since the guys had laughed at him before. What they did not realize is that their ridicule of him had made him angry enough to inflict serious harm to one of them, but he had managed to control his tongue.

Even though Clemis resented being derided, he could not seem to relinquish his dream of marrying one of the school teachers. Even though he wanted to, he could not seem to get a grasp on his compulsion to talk about the teachers incessantly to anyone who would listen. He carried on about them so much that some folk in Hawk Town began to wonder if Clemis was on the verge of losing his mind.

Marie and Madesyn had also begun to become a bit more uneasy about Clemis' sudden appearances, and the frequency with which he visited them. He had developed a habit of dropping by the school almost on a daily basis while the children were having lunch and mid-day recess. Clemis would bring fruits, nuts— peanuts, pecans, and walnuts—depending upon the season, to dole out to the kids and teachers. While the teachers felt it would be rude to refuse Clemis' offerings, as politely as possible they attempted to discourage him. But Clemis was not a man to be dissuaded. As a matter of fact, he thought the ladies attempt to put him off was actually a "come on." In his warped way of thinking, he believed both teachers were falling in love with him. Clemis knew he had a decision to make. He was going to have to break one of the teacher's hearts whenever he decided to let them know which one of them he had chosen to be his wife and mother of his children.

Marie and Madesyn had become so concerned about Clemis' frequent visits to the school that when the superintendent paid one of his monthly assessment visits to the school, they voiced their concern and asked the superintendent if he would speak to Clemis about disrupting the teachers' daily schedule for the children.

When Mr. Kenneth Monroe, the District Superintendent, held a conference with Clemis, Clemis appeared to have understood clearly. However, Clemis was slowly developing odious feelings toward Mr. Monroe, whom heretofore he seemed to have liked. Clemis wondered whether Mr. Monroe himself had eyes for the new school teachers. Well, Clemis was not going to let Mr. Monroe and his silly request prevent him from wooing Madesyn, whom he had decided was the better woman for him. There was nothing wrong with Marie except she was the older of the two women. Not to be outdone, Clemis began dropping by the teachers' bungalow after school almost daily. He might not have been able to stop by the school house, but Mr. Monroe could not stop him from visiting the ladies at home.

***

Buster's Place was a 32-by-32-square-foot wood-frame structure with a lean-to front and back porches. The wood had never been painted inside or outside, so the building itself looked rustic, drab, and weather-beaten. Several wooden benches lined the north and south interior walls, and a few old wooden chairs were scattered about on the back porch. There was a porch swing out front, inviting weary souls to sit and sway back and forth, nod or chat, depending upon the circumstances or situations as espoused by community folks. In other words, whatever hot topic there was to gossip about, in all likelihood, bits and pieces of it could be heard on the front porch of Buster's Place. An old rocker stood on one side of the front door, and was usually occupied by the evening's first visitor.

Buster was Clemis' best customer because Buster sold drinks to all who came looking to unwind after a hard day's work. Although on Wednesday night the men who lived in the Hawk Town area of Kinder County dominated Buster's Place while their wives attended the Bible Study and Prayer meeting, on the weekends the scene at Buster's was totally different. The place was full of not only older men, but young men, loose women, and young unsupervised girls also would sneak out and could be seen hanging out in the dark. Too often, dirty old men would pay some of the innocent young girls to lie down with them. And one of the so-called big secrets among school-age girls was that an easy way to make good money in a bad way was to sneak over to Buster's Place, which was foreign to their prim and proper wives.

When or if a young girl became a "regular" for a certain Mr. Wanna B. Bigshot at Buster's Place, she no longer had to perform the menial chores of farm life. She could rely on performing acts for her newly found Mr. Goodbar or Sugar Daddy and never have to set foot in the fields again. There was a tremendous amount of these secret rendezvous filling the nights all over Kinder County. But Peggy, for lack of mobility, could only observe the happenings around Buster's place because it was within walking distance from her special hiding place in the Hawk Town woods.

Only a few miles down the road from the community hangout was Miss Circe's Place, known to many adults as a house of ill repute. Circe was really not the owner's name. Actually, the owner's name was Roxanne, who was a libertine and operated the house known as Miss Circe's Place. She was sometimes shunned because of the kind of action that was said to take place behind those closed doors. Peggy was too young to even take a look inside. The way her daddy talked about the women who lived there, he would have died a natural death if his baby girl had ever dreamed of going in that wicked place. Peggy had heard Clemis on numerous occasions refer to Miss Circe's Place as a hoe (whore) house. But Peggy could not, for the life of herself, grasp the reason for the fury that boiled from Clemis when he mentioned the place. Clemis kept their hoes at the shed next door to their smoke house. It was a tiny shed, but big enough to keep all 12 of their hoes out of the weather. And as far as Peggy could tell, her daddy never got mad about the hoes they kept. So what was different about the hoes at Miss Circe's Place? Peggy wanted so much to see them, if for nothing more but to figure out the reason behind Clemis' distress. After all, and furthermore, the women who sat on the big screened-in porch at Miss Circe's Place didn't even have a garden to chop. As a matter of fact, Peggy never saw them do any work. They just sat around and looked pretty all the time.

Well, there had to be some big secret that they were keeping, and Peggy was determined to one day discover what it was, if for no other reason except to find a way to keep her daddy calm when he talked about those hoes. Clemis was adamant when he talked about those hoes with his eldest son, Teddy. He told Teddy to stay away from that place. On more than one occasion, Peggy had heard Clemis say to Teddy, "Never go there, boy! Do you hear me?" But Peggy had never heard Clemis mention Miss Circe's place to his eldest daughter, Cora.

***

All things considered, Clemis presumed himself to be some privileged character because of his long standing superficially friendly relationship with Sheriff Zack Green. Actually, from the sheriff's perspective, the relationship was nothing more than a convenient association with a blowhard. For Clemis to believe that Sheriff Zack Green was his friend was implausible for most community folks, but Clemis was unconcerned about what the neighbors and associates thought of his dealings with the sheriff. Clemis customarily spouted off some circumlocution to exaggerate his importance, while those in his presence hardly listened to what they considered meaningless blabber.

In reality, Clemis' dealings with the sheriff could not be dismissed as insignificant because Zack Green, unbeknownst to community folks, was another one of Clemis' best customers. Their transactions were made late at night while most residents of Hawk Town were asleep. But there was one little person who often heard and saw what the two men so carefully tried to conceal. Clemis' baby girl, Peggy, although only 8 years old, had a keen sense of her surroundings and was gifted with unbelievable extrasensory perception. Moreover, Peggy was unusual in that her brain and body required very little sleep, so she was often awake at night, using her senses to encapsulate activity in her surroundings. Therefore, many supposedly secrets of the night were no secrets at all to Peggy. She often saw the exchanges between her daddy and the sheriff as turgid. But she knew that her daddy's bootleg alcohol was part of the glue that held her family together.

From her secret hiding place, she would see the wad of money the sheriff put in her daddy's pocket. She knew that their dirty dealings were not done helter-skelter because there was a pattern to the manner in which they operated.

At certain times during the month, Clemis would put 24 jars of his product in the smokehouse. Twelve jars of wine and 12 jars of liquor. She heard them call it stump hole and sometimes they called it moonshine, but she did not know why. She wondered whether or not the term "moonshine" was used because the transactions with this liquid always took place at night. Peggy didn't dwell on trying to deduce the origin of the term "stump hole" because nothing about the shenanigans she observed could be applied to the term according to her way of thinking. She wondered why anyone would pay for something that tasted so awful. She knew it had a horrible taste because she had sneaked into the smokehouse one evening and took a swig. At that moment, Peggy decided that thereafter she would only taste the wine.

Some nights when there was no moon visible in the sky, Clemis would go out to the smokehouse at midnight. In a minute or two later, Sheriff Zack Green would drive up to the smokehouse with his car's head lights turned off. Peggy could hear him coming at least a mile away. She knew the sound of his vehicle. Who else would dare ride around in the dark with no headlights beaming at midnight? Most neighbors and people of the community didn't even own a vehicle, except maybe a few farmers who owned farm tractors. And they reserved the fuel that was required to operate their machinery only when necessary for farm-related chores and activities.

After those midnight rendezvous, Clemis always appeared to be in a good mood. Perhaps it was because he had a pocket full of money, thanks to good ole Zack.

Those episodes were the only time Peggy had ever observed Clemis taking a slug of his own liquor. Because most of the time he only drank at Buster's Place.

Peggy was mystified as to why the two men found it necessary to meet secretively at night to make those particular exchanges, but otherwise shared an open relationship in the presence of community folks. While she was curious about their midnight dealings, her instincts told her it would be a colossal mistake to question her daddy about those louche meetings. Peggy had always been taught that honesty was a wonderful thing if you could afford it. And she felt that in this case her daddy could not afford to be honest. She knew that the sheriff was no paragon because she had heard her older sister, Daisy, and eldest brother, Teddy, whispering about the kind of things Sheriff Green and Miss Esther, over near the creek bottom, engaged in when they thought everyone was at work and the kids were at school. Why those two, it was rumored, even had a baby together. Peggy believed it because the boy, Casper, was very light-skinned and had straight hair like Sheriff Green, even though Miss Esther and Mr. Johnny, Casper's alleged biological father, were both dark-skinned with kinky hair.

Mr. Johnny was quite a character himself. Rumor was that he knew that Sheriff Zack Green was balling his wife, but he was having an affair, too, so he did not have time to dwell on the wretched behavior of Miss Esther and the sheriff. Mr. Johnny was vehemently attracted to a promiscuous woman named Delilah, who without a doubt, lived up to the name. Delilah was married to a humble, hard-working man named Briscoe Jones. He was a handsome man whose good looks often caught the eyes of a great many ladies, but Briscoe was so blinded by his love for Delilah that he never gave any noticeable attention to the flirtatious women who seemed to always be looking to strip a man of his clothes and his wallet—mostly his wallet.

Invariably, almost every morning after Briscoe left for the mile-long walk to his job, and the Jones children left for school, Mr. Johnny could be seen hastily making his way to the Jones home. Mr. Johnny didn't have to knock once he reached the door because Delilah habitually kept the door unlocked. As a matter of fact, most people in Hawk Town kept their doors unlocked, day and night. The sight of Delilah in the black negligee that he had given her as a Christmas gift never failed to increase the fires burning in Mr. Johnny's loins from red hot to white hot. He held no misgivings about romping in the bed in which Briscoe had slept peacefully with Delilah only a few hours before. Once his desire for Delilah had been temporarily satiated, he always left the Jones residence and headed for Buster's Place. It was usually around lunch time before Delilah had finished fornicating and schmoozing Mr. Johnny, so by this time, all the boys (old men) of the neighborhood were arriving at Buster's for their usual lunchtime chatter.

One of the things the older men bragged about to one another more than anything else was their female conquests. So, Mr. Johnny and Delilah's affair was no secret among the boys. It was simply another bit of fodder for the discussion whenever sex was the focus of their conversation. They often laughed about Briscoe Jones' naïve ignorance when it came to his wife's promiscuous ways. Because while Mr. Johnny appeared to be the chosen one to extinguish her flames at the moment, several of the boys had fulfilled that same pleasurable task in previous years.

What none of the gang realized was that even though Briscoe Jones seemed to be blind to Delilah's insatiable desire to have her fires smoldered by other men, he was keenly aware of the sex gumbo that she cooked up with other men of the community. Briscoe knew what Mr. Johnny was doing with his wife. It bothered him so much that he had become a shadow of the man he used to be. But no one seemed to notice. However, inwardly Briscoe was battling the urge to take some action to end the charade of calmness he outwardly displayed. He was fed up with the humiliation for himself, and especially for his children who were ridiculed constantly about their mother's lack of an acceptable moral compass.

One day Briscoe's anger had built up to such a crescendo that he knew this was the day he was going to end it all. He was going to take care of Delilah, Mr. Johnny, and himself. He had tolerated the situation for years because his children were young and dependent upon him. But now his eldest daughter, Joyce, was a senior in high school with only one month left until graduation. She was physically strong and a strong-willed girl, and Briscoe knew that she was now quite capable of caring for her two younger siblings. So the time was ripe for a showdown.

On the morning destined for disaster, Briscoe left for work at the usual time in his usual fashion. But instead of walking the mile to his job, he veered into the woods at a spot where he had hidden his shotgun the night before. Yes, he thought to himself, this is premeditated, but who cares? When enough time had passed that he knew Mr. Johnny would be headed to his (Briscoe's) home, Briscoe became robotically still and remained church-mouse quiet. He watched Mr. Johnny breeze along on the way to cavort with Delilah. Briscoe became so incensed that he could hardly contain himself; he could hardly breathe. But he knew he had to control his impulse to shoot Mr. Johnny right there on the spot because he had to actually catch Mr. Johnny and Delilah in the act before the action he was going to take could be justified in his mind, and by a jury of his peers, if it reached that point. So, he waited.

When Mr. Johnny opened the unlocked door and entered the Jones residence, there stood Delilah, looking luscious in the all too familiar black negligee that Mr. Johnny loved ogling. While Delilah gave him her usual sultry smile, Mr. Johnny was rushing to loosen his belt and unzip the fly of his trousers. He could not wait to get to the bedroom to sink into the pool of pleasure that Delilah always offered him so freely. When she fell onto her back, gapped her legs open, and licked her voluptuous lips, Mr. Johnny was dead to all the world except to the pleasure he was anticipating as he plowed deep into Delilah's warmth. Delilah and Mr. Johnny were so engrossed in their wild ride of torrid passion that they did not hear Briscoe enter the house. As Briscoe stood just outside the bedroom threshold bristling with a rage so intense that his whole body shook violently, he could hardly raise the shotgun to aim in the direction of the moans and groans that the two lovers elicited as they romped around in Briscoe's bed. Mr. Johnny and Delilah were enraptured with the pleasurable sensations that had augmented their fornicating for more than a year. Their bodies were sweaty and their minds were closed to everything except the pleasure they were relishing from each other.

***

At exactly 11:30 that morning, Peggy was playing outside when she heard two loud booms. She had no way of knowing that the sound was coming from the blasts of Briscoe Jones' shotgun, so she thought little of it. She knew the sound of shotgun blasts because men hunted in the area all winter, and this time of year people shot snakes and other pests that got in the way, or an animal that would become supper. Peggy assumed, incorrectly of course, that another neighbor had just obtained supper meat for his family. But a short while after hearing the booming sounds, Peggy heard a popping sound that reminded her of the sound made whenever Clemis was out back target shooting with his .380 caliber pistol. For the remainder of the day it was relatively quiet until the kids traipsed along at the end of the school day. It had to be around 3:45 in the afternoon when Peggy heard a gut-wrenching scream. The sound was coming from the direction of the Jones' house.

A few minutes later, Joyce Jones was seen running like a gazelle coming up the road. She was screaming and crying uncontrollably as neighbors were charging to her rescue to see what had upset the girl so much. When Joyce could catch her breath and speak with some semblance of clarity, she hiccupped enough words to explain that her mother, father, and Mr. Johnny were all dead inside her house. Daisy, being the oldest female around at the moment, took Joyce by the hand and led her inside Daisy's home where she sat with Joyce and hugged her gently.

In the meantime, five or six adults went running to the Jones residence. It was Clemis who told everyone to stand back from the scene, and he ordered his son Teddy to go quickly and find the sheriff and bring him back at once. Everyone was in a state of shock. It was apparent that a catastrophe had clouded over the usual sunny community of Hawk Town. For a brief spell, silence was deafening while everyone waited for the sheriff. No one dared speak a word. The atmosphere could be likened to a "wake" before the official wake.

Somehow, Miss Circe had heard the news and came to offer her sympathy to the Jones children. The two younger girls had not made it home from school, and couldn't yet know about the tragedy that would change the course of their lives forever. They were about to step from an orderly, structured world into one that was going to be chaotic and amorphous.

When Miss Circe learned that the two younger children were still at school, she ordered her driver to take her to the school at once. There, she beckoned Marie and Madesyn aside and explained the events of the day that had unhinged the Jones family. Although the two teachers were reluctant to do so, they instructed the two Jones girls to go with Miss Circe. Marie told the children that their sister was waiting for them at Clemis Stapleton's home. Without asking any questions, the children went along innocently because they were excited over the opportunity to ride in Miss Circe's big pretty Cadillac. Miss Circe was thinking about how beautiful the three Jones girls were. They had all been fortunate enough to be blessed with Delilah's good looks. Miss Circe was thinking that one day they might be a prized addition to her harem of wanton women. Although she had plans to give the girls a good home if Kinder County officials would let her, she knew that community folks would offer resistance due to the nature of her business. But she was willing to fight for custody of the girls. They had no known relatives in the area and Miss Circe knew that financially she was in much better shape to provide for the girls than most of the prim and proper citizens of Kinder County. Most were not willing to spend their hard- earned money to help a neighbor or a stranger. So, Miss Circe figured this fact alone gave her the upper hand in what would be an upcoming custody battle for the girls.

By the time Miss Circe and the two Jones girls arrived at the Stapleton residence, Joyce had calmed down a bit and was sitting catatonically, seemingly staring into space. Upon seeing her two younger sisters, she made a quick transition from a state of numbness to loving caretaker. She hugged her two siblings with a crushing squeeze that left the girls almost breathless. The girls asked simultaneously what was wrong because they sensed that Joyce was extremely upset. Joyce was not acting like the sister that they knew so well. In order to prevent amplification of the horrific situation, Daisy Stapleton told the girls that something had happened to their parents and they needed to be strong together. Daisy reassured the girls that they were among friends and everyone was going to help in every way they could. The girls were told not to worry.

"But what's wrong?" cried Annie, the older of the two young girls. "What has happened to Mom and Dad?" Daisy's sense of compassion was strong, but momentarily she was at a loss for words to console the girls. But she quickly recovered and stammered that Rev. Herman, their pastor, had been notified and was on his way there. She told them that Rev. Herman would explain and offer them special comfort directly from God. Then the room fell silent again.

***

Over at the Jones residence Sheriff Green and two young detectives were busy attempting to sort out the sequence of events that had led to this tragedy. It appeared that Briscoe had come home and found Mr. Johnny in bed with Delilah, and had shot both of them with his shotgun at close range. And then he had committed suicide with his .380 pistol. There was blood spatter all over the bedroom. Upon initial observation of the gory sight, one of the young detectives who was relatively new in his position lost his breakfast. He stood in a corner of the room hyperventilating from the shock of it all. Sheriff Green described the scene as the worst he had ever encountered in all the 26 years he had served in law enforcement in Kinder County.

The bodies could neither be moved from their positions nor removed from the Jones home until the coroner had made his assessment. This was going to take a while because the coroner, John Riverbank, who served three contiguous counties, was in another county working on a case where a 12-year old boy had drowned in a creek near his parents' farm. John Riverbank was also fairly new in his position as coroner. John was a pathologist with an undergraduate degree in biochemistry who also had earned a medical degree. Being qualified to conduct autopsies made John a prize catch for Kinder and the surrounding counties. He had recently graduated from Harvard University and returned home to serve in the region where he had grown up. Initially, he had been surprised to find himself involved in so many cases in what he had heretofore considered slow, easy, and peaceful southern living compared to the northern cities in which he had lived in during his years at Harvard. The situation being convoluted as it was, the most pressing problem at the moment for the Jones girls was where they would spend the night.

Since Miss Circe had offered to take the girls home to her big house where there was a huge empty bedroom that the three girls could share; and since there obviously was no room at the Stapleton home because there were 11 children living in three bedrooms already; and since no one else had stepped forward and offered to take the girls home with them, the social worker who had just arrived and was assessing the situation had a serious decision to make. Although her moral compass was pointing toward strong disapproval because she felt great disdain for Miss Circe's house of ill repute, momentarily she offered no objection to an overnight stay at Miss Circe's big house. Because, from experience, she knew that in all of Kinder County there was no other available space with anyone who would consider housing the three Jones girls. The social worker made it clear that she would be working relentlessly to make better, more acceptable, temporary provisions for the girls until permanent placement arrangements could be made.

Since the social worker could not immediately parse out a more immediate suitable solution in this case, it was settled for the moment that Miss Circe would take the girls. The two younger girls were elated over the decision. They had always wanted to get a look inside Miss Circe's Place because their mom had told them that was where she had lived before she had met and married their dad. Joyce, however, was a bit concerned because she had heard so many ugly rumors about Miss Circe's Place and what went on there. Noticing the look of concern on Joyce's face, Miss Circe promised Joyce that they would be safe. She assured Joyce that no one was going to lay a hand on her or her sisters.

Before they could continue the conversation, Rev. Herman arrived. After making his pleasantries, he asked to speak to the three girls privately. And once they were alone, he explained to the two younger girls, without going into details, that something terrible had happened, and their mom and dad were now going to live in Heaven. Rev. Herman assured the girls that their parents loved them. He told them they now had two guardian angels who would always be watching over them and protecting them.

No one noticed that Rev. Herman's hands were shaking and that his shirt was stuck to his back. Not because of the weather, because it wasn't that hot. And not because he had run to the Jones residence, because he arrived in his chauffeur-driven Ford. Rev. Herman was nervous and upset because he was remembering the times he, himself, had sneaked to Briscoe Jones' home and lay with Delilah before he married his wife, Emily, and before Mr. Johnny had begun to seek pleasure from Delilah. Secretly, Rev. Herman was thanking God that Briscoe had not doubled back home one of those mornings a few years back.

Rev. Herman was no saint. Actually, he could best be described as a Lothario. And his position as a minister provided many opportunities for him to engage in unacceptable seductive behaviors with more than several women of his church. Even though he lacked reverence, he frowned upon the idea of the Jones girls going to live, albeit temporarily, with Miss Circe. Because in the wee hours of the morning when Miss Emily thought Rev. Herman was traveling home on his way from preaching a long-distance sermon, Rev. Herman was sinning and loving it at Miss Circe's Place. It was a known fact that Rev. Herman was a regular who had no particular favorite at Miss Circe's. Whoever was available when he could steal away suited Rev. Herman just fine. Because Rev. Herman was thinking he could not risk having the Jones girls see this dark side of his character that he enjoyed so well and could never give up, he was concerned about the Jones girls living with Miss Circe. In his mind all of the women had something special to offer. And he was always saying, "Variety is the spice of life." He did not practice what he preached.

He disobeyed more than a few of the Ten Commandments. He committed adultery and loved it. He coveted other men's wives and was not ashamed of it. He did not love his neighbors and he did not care, because as far as he was concerned, he did not have to be tolerant of people who had lost their way in life. And his neighbors appeared to be a passel of humans who had lost their way.

All things considered, Rev. Herman kept his opinion to himself relative to the Jones girls and their newly proposed living arrangement. He would simply have to exercise extreme caution from now on when he ventured to Miss Circe's Place.

When Miss Circe and the girls arrived at her big house, her ladies of ill repute made a big fuss over the young virgins. They were eager to show Joyce and her little sisters around the place. They began the tour in the kitchen because Miss Circe and the girls had entered in the back foyer. The kitchen was a huge eat-in rectangular-shaped room with a bank of windows on the east wall that captured the daily sunrise. They were decorated with white lace curtains. The paint of choice was chartreuse, which was a perfect choice for the kitchen. The huge rectangular oak table in the center of the room was large enough to seat 12 consumers at any given setting—breakfast, lunch, or dinner. Two large stoves, two refrigerators, and cabinets covered the space on the remaining walls. Two of the cabinets contained sinks. The girls stood open mouthed at the sight of it all. They had always felt that Miss Circe's Place was beautiful, but had no idea it was this magnificent. As they were shown room after room, their feeling was this house exuded "je ne sais quoi."

Finally, the girls were settled into their large bedroom, which by all standards could be considered a suite because they had their own private bathroom and a large sitting area. There was one double bed and a set of twin beds—perfect for Joyce and her two younger sisters.

***

Two miles away, in the section of Hawk Town that mostly resembled a town, the old undertaker, Zollie Richardson, was figuring on how much he would profit from handling the three bodies. It had been a year and a half since death brought him a body, so he was nearly drooling over the fact that there would be some extra money in his pockets after having gone through a long dry spell. And his wife, Ophelia, was already planning a trip to the city where she would indulge herself with that new red suit she had been eyeballing ever since it had been on display at Angie's Fashion Shoppe. Ophelia had big plans for spending Zollie's money as fast, or faster, than he could make it.

***

The day of the funeral arrived all too soon for the grieving Jones girls. It was a blue-sky day with a cool southwest wind that was welcomed by what appeared to be a sea of people--mourners, gossipers, trouble-makers, and sad-faced children. They were waiting outside the church hoping to get and up close and personal glimpse of the bereaved family before entering the church.

Back at Miss Circe's Place, Joyce had to muster a show of strength for her little sisters. The closer it came to the appointed hour, Joyce felt her strength melting away. Miss Circe, being the perceptive madam that she was, placed her arm around Joyce's shoulder in a gesture of comfort that was very touching—so touching that Joyce could no longer hold back the tears. She nearly had a meltdown—releasing all the pent-up sorrow she had been holding inside since the day she found her parents and Mr. Johnny dead. It was a tragic experience that she would never be able to erase from her memory bank.

It was a three-mile drive to Mt. Mercy Methodist Church. Zollie Richardson's Cadillac limousine arrived promptly at Miss Circe's Place at the appointed time, 12:30 p.m. The funeral service was scheduled to begin at 1 o'clock. The cortege leaving Miss Circe's Place was not very long. The lead vehicle was Zollie's Cadillac limousine, followed by Rev. Herman's chauffeur-driven Ford, Clemis Stapleton's old Chevrolet pickup truck, and Sheriff Zack Brown bringing up the rear in his sheriff department's cruiser.

Clemis was expressing condolences primarily because his children and the Jones girls had a close friendship. He was at a loss as to what to do except be there with his older children. It was customary for Sheriff Zack Green to be seen at the tail end of a funeral cortege. In his mind, that was one of his self-appointed official duties.

A funeral in Hawk Town was a grand event. All the country folk traditionally stopped work to attend the service. The school day always ended at 12 noon on the day of a funeral so that older children could attend if they so desired. Outside the church people were waiting and socializing and chatting in whispered voices. Most of the adults were dressed in black attire. The exception was seen in the ladies who had agreed to serve as floral attendants, and the ushers of Mt. Mercy Methodist Church. They were all dressed in white.

Once the vehicles in the cortege had parked in front of Mt. Mercy, Sheriff Zack Green left immediately. Miss Esther was one of the few Hawk Town individuals not attending the funeral because she knew that on funeral days, she had other fish to fry. She and Zack Green had established this pattern of sneaking some stolen moments whenever there was a funeral going on, and they had carried on in this fashion for years. While everyone was at church and would be there for four or five hours, Zack Green was going to take advantage of the fact that he could sneak over and rendezvous with Miss Esther, his half-black baby's mama. The sheriff knew he had to be careful with his lovemaking because he did not want another slip up. He could not afford to have another child upsetting his wife. Shirley had gone nearly out of her mind when she first heard through the grapevine about the sheriff's little black boy, Casper.

***

In the beginning when they were a newly wedded couple, Sheriff Green and Shirley were relentless in their effort to start a family. Shirley had always dreamed of having four children—two boys and two girls. But as the years passed and she never conceived, she began to experience bouts of depression and, consequently, Zack and her once close relationship began to crumble. Shirley turned to ladies' clubs and Bible Study for comfort, and Zack Green turned to Miss Esther.

After fornicating over a period of time, Miss Esther informed Zack that she was pregnant with his child. She knew that Mr. Johnny was not its father because she and Mr. Johnny had not had sexual intercourse in more than a year. Mr. Johnny sought his pleasure from other women, but mostly from Delilah, and Miss Esther did not care because Zack Green was satisfying all of her sexual desires.

Nine years before, Zack had been confounded by the news that he was going to be a father. But in the midst of his astonishment, secretly he was happy. Because over the years he had begun to think he might be infertile—that it was his fault that Shirley never got pregnant. But he and his wife had never discussed that possibility. She just solemnly accepted the fact that she was barren, and she and Zack resigned themselves with verity that they would never be parents.

Armed with the knowledge that he was going to have a child, Zack could not have been happier except for the problem of keeping this secret from Shirley. But everyone knows that so-called secrets in a small town or the rural country is the ultimate confabulator of juicy gossip. So all it would take was one trip to the doctor and word would spread like wildfire about Miss Esther's condition. And the first question to be asked would be "Who is the father?" The unanimous response would be, "Sheriff Zack Green!" Even though people were thinking it was bound to have happened, compassionate souls were going to feel sorry for Shirley, Zack's wife.

There is always some tongue-wagger dying to spill the beans to the individual who would be most seriously wounded by the news, and in Hawk Town that person was none other than Miss Hattie Strut. Once she heard the news, she could hardly wait for Wednesday night Bible Study so she could begin the discussion of the Seventh Commandment—"Thou Shalt Not Commit Adultery." By any means possible, Miss Hattie was going to make sure Shirley knew about Miss Esther's condition. With alleged knowledge of the pregnancy, Hattie Strut figured Shirley could draw her own conclusions as to who the father might be.

***

Casper was a humble, polite child. He knew he was different because the other kids always teased him about his straight hair and his very light, almost white, skin. Although no one had ever told him, he believed that Sheriff Green was his biological father. Heck, he looked like the sheriff, and Sheriff Green was always sneaking over to his house when everyone thought Casper was at school. During those times, Casper knew that his daddy, Mr. Johnny, was not at home, so Sheriff Green had to be visiting his mother, Miss Esther. Casper skipped school a lot and hid out in the woods near his home until the school day ended. He didn't like being teased and shunned at school. Peggy Stapleton was his best friend at school, and on the days that Peggy was absent from school, Casper would never enter the schoolhouse door. Some days he and Peggy would play hooky together and hang out at the creek and fish all day. Some days they would hide in the woods near Miss Circe's Place to see who was visiting those licentious women.

***

All the gawkers who had been waiting outside for a close-up glimpse of Joyce and her sisters began to file into the sanctuary searching for positions on a pew that would give them a bird's eye view of the grieving family. From his vantage point on the opposite side of the sanctuary, as Teddy watched Joyce he was captivated by her breathtaking beauty. Moreover, Joyce's disposition was of a quiet, calm nature, but today she appeared to be overcome by sadness. Teddy wondered if she and her sisters were safe at Miss Circe's Place because untold numbers of dirty old men who frequented the place might attempt to put their dirty old hands on the pretty young virgins.

Suddenly, Teddy was overcome with the urge to protect Joyce and her sisters. He began to think that if he were in a position to do so, he would ask for Joyce's hand in marriage. But now there was no family member to ask because both of Joyce's parents were now deceased. Nevertheless, even if there was someone to ask, he had nothing of substance to offer Joyce. He believed his love for Joyce was strong enough to withstand the test of time, but he needed something more than he had to offer her. He thought about the money he had saved over the years to be used for him to escape the lackluster doldrums of Hawk Town. His savings were going to give him a better life than he had at home helping Clemis on the farm. But now he was thinking he could use the money to purchase the old Martin house that has been for sale for nearly two years now. It was solid and in immaculate condition. The home offered three bedrooms and had been built in the

1930s when only the best virgin lumber had been used in the construction industry. Old Lady Martin had maintained her home with tender loving care until she passed away two years ago.

The Martin property was contiguous to Teddy's family homestead, which meant he would still be available to keep an eye on his younger siblings, as well as lend a helping hand to his daddy whenever he was needed. Although he might find it difficult to fit all essential activities of two households within a 24-hour period on a daily basis, he felt strongly that he would be able to manage fairly well. He had never shied away from a challenge. Now, all he needed to do was keep his thoughts to himself to prolong the time Joyce needed to grieve the loss of her parents and adjust to a new lifestyle. After all, her role in life had suddenly undergone a drastic change. In the meantime, Teddy would check on Joyce and her siblings at every opportunity to ensure that no one was attempting to take advantage of them.

***

When Rev. Herman began to preach the eulogy, Mrs. Herman's eyes slowly moved in the direction of Rose Hill, who she believed was having an affair with her husband. And surely enough, there sat Rose drooling at the lips, licking and twisting on the pew as if she was ready for a romp with Rev. Herman right then and there. Mrs. Herman (she was also known as First Lady Herman) had to fight the urge to go over and slap Rose with a force that would have knocked her into next week.

As Joyce sat listening to Rev. Herman eulogize her parents, she was wondering how she was going to cope with her incredulous family situation. Although her daddy had promised her that she would be able to attend college in the fall, she knew that was an impossibility now that she had sole responsibility for caring for her two younger sisters. She could never leave them and go away—not after the tremendous loss they had just suffered. And she definitely would not leave her sisters to live with Miss Circe without her being there to protect them.

Joyce could have been paralyzed with grief temporarily because she was enveloped by acute emotional pain, but she had to boldly and courageously face the future, without pause, because she was ultimately the sole caretaker for her younger sisters. And she was determined to provide the best possible upbringing, under the circumstances, that they could ever have. She planned to see that they completed their education through high school, and she would find a way to help them go to college if that's what they wanted to do when they graduated.

Joyce, lost in thought, sensed that someone on the opposite side of the sanctuary was staring at her. She stole a glimpse across the crowded pews and, surely enough, there was the secret love she daydreamed about—Teddy. He was actually staring in her direction. She gave him a sweet, shy smile and quickly turned back to face Rev. Herman. Now, she became lost in thoughts of Teddy. She wondered what it would be like to spend the rest of her life with him as his wife. She thought about the money that had been saved for her college education. She was thinking that since the notion of college had been nullified with her parents' death, she could use some of the money for a simple wedding dress if only Teddy would propose marriage to her. She wondered what her mother would think about this idea. Then she felt she was being silly. Teddy had never even indicated that he had special feelings for her—which meant her daydreaming was ridiculously off base.

Rev. Herman was ending the eulogy with a prayer. After which the choir sang a rendition of "This World Is Not My Home." As the recessional exited the church, the mood was far less somber than it had been prior to the service. A lot of chatter could be heard as friends who had not seen each other in a while exclaimed "hellos" and hugged one another as if this might be the last time they would ever see one another. Teddy inched his way through the crowd until he reached Joyce, who was standing next to Miss Circe's limousine. He spoke first— expressing his heartfelt sympathy. He asked Joyce if there was anything he could help her with. Joyce seemed reluctant to respond, so Teddy used the lull in conversation to ask Joyce if he might come visit her at Miss Circe's on Sunday after church. Joyce said she needed to first clear it with Miss Circe, but told Teddy that she would love to have him visit her on Sunday. She asked Teddy to wait in that very spot while she got permission from Miss Circe. She found Miss Circe chatting with Rev. Herman and asked her if it would be alright if Teddy Stapleton paid her a visit on Sunday after worship service. Miss Circe nodded her approval. When she returned to Teddy, she told him that Miss Circe had given her approval. Teddy thanked Joyce and told her he could not remain at the church fellowship hall to dine with the family. Joyce understood and waved at Teddy as he left the church yard. He was feeling euphoric.

Clemis had been watching and listening to the exchange between Teddy and Joyce. He wondered what his eldest son had in mind because Joyce was so young. He vowed that before he slept a wink that night he was going to be sure to ask Teddy about his plans.

***

Now that Mr. Johnny had met his Waterloo, Sheriff Green was concerned that the primary breadwinner of the Brown household had been killed. Even though he avoided his son, Casper, he loved him and did not want him to suffer hunger pains or lack any of the basic necessities for activities of daily living, however minimal. Sheriff Green knew he was going to have to give more of his bounty to Miss Esther for little Casper's sake.

Casper had never seen the sheriff at Miss Circe's Place. Perhaps he had missed him. But Casper knew that most of the Hawk Town men visited Miss Circe's at one time or another. Although Casper had never seen Sheriff Green at Miss Circe's Place, he had seen him at his home, visiting his mother, on numerous occasions. The few times he had come in contact with Sheriff Green, the sheriff had always been nice to him. Zack Green would ask him insignificant questions such as how he was doing in school, did he like playing ball, what did he want to be when he grew up, and so forth. One time Sheriff Green asked him if he had ever been to the drugstore in Dillington and drunk a soda from the fountain. Casper told him that he had not.

At school one day a few weeks following that conversation and inquiry, the Misses Marie and Madesyn told all five kids in the fourth grade that they were going to town to visit the drugstore and drink a soda from the fountain. The teachers said this was because all five fourth-graders had scored 100 on their semester exam. Marie and Madesyn told them at that time that Rev. Herman would be driving them to town in his little old church bus. The church bus was actually a small older school bus that had been re-painted a shade of blue and sold by the Kinder County School Board to Mt. Mercy Church for $1. Miss Madesyn would be chaperoning the trip while Miss Marie remained at school with the other children. The teachers told the entire student body that from that day forward, if all students in any class scored 100 on the semester exam, the entire class would get a field trip to Dillington to sightsee and visit the drugstore for a fountain soda. When Casper arrived from school that day very excited and told Miss Esther about the upcoming field trip, she hardly seemed surprised. She already knew that Casper was a child of academic excellence, and his daddy, Sheriff Zack Green, was a rogue.

***

In the weeks following the funeral services of the three deceased victims, the deaths of Mr. and Mrs. Briscoe Jones, along with that of Mr. Johnny Brown, had taken its toll on everyone at school. The children were lamenting while their two teachers continued to say silent prayers for God's comfort for the Jones girls. Everyone appeared to be getting through daily routines in robotic fashion.

During the evenings at the teachers' cottage, in addition to sound of silence, the sounds of pages turning, pencils being sharpened, the tea kettle whistling, and light footsteps periodically walking across the kitchen floor were all that wafted through the air.

Not having a clue of the danger they were in, the catastrophic event that was currently dominating the talk of Hawk Town would pale in comparison to an event that was looming around the corner due to Marie and Madesyn's naïveté. Because back at the Stapleton home, a storm was brewing. Clemis had a desperate hankering to bring a wife into his home to care for his rambunctious children. And he had conjured up the notion almost a year ago that he was going to marry Miss Madesyn—the younger school teacher. He decided he would give her just a bit more time to settle down from the disastrous situation that had befallen the Joneses and Mr. Johnny. But, he was thinking, she had better get over it quickly because his patience had worn thin. He had noticed how Teddy had been eyeballing the eldest Jones girl, and Clemis figured his son would soon be courting her and getting married. He also felt that his eldest daughter, Cora, would be leaving home with the first young man that asked for her hand in marriage. He felt that she was tired of the motherly role that had been thrust upon her when her mother passed away almost 10 years ago. Dorothy had died in childbirth when their daughter Peggy, who was now almost 9 years old, was born.

Clemis was getting worked up into a frenzy as he anticipated the future possibilities. Whenever he was in this frame of mind, he always yearned to talk about his feelings, but there was no one with whom he felt close enough to that he could share his inner feelings. During such times, he tended to venture over to Buster's Place simply to be in the presence of other men his age, even though he did not drink regularly or gamble with them anymore. And he certainly did not keep company with the floozies (as he thought of them) that frequented Buster's Place. But he needed to be heard. He was bursting with an inner excitement relative to marrying Miss Madesyn Moore.

On this particular evening, Randy--one of Buster's regular customers who was known all over Hawk Town for his big mouth, and whose tongue got more loose the more he drank—was already three sheets to the wind when Clemis arrived at 7 o'clock that particular Wednesday evening. Randy immediately began asking Clemis a series of personal questions. "How's the family?" "Whatcha been up to these days? You haven't found a gal you want to take care of your children yet?" That last question gave Clemis the opening he needed to release some of the pent- up emotional pressure that had been mushrooming in him over the past year.

"As a matter of fact, I have," Clemis replied. "I'm going to marry myself a school teacher." Prior to making the statement to Randy, Clemis had said to himself that he would guard his speech about his impending plans to get married, even though he was so excited that he could hardly suppress his emotions. However, he had lost control and let the words flow freely out of his mouth as soon as Randy had begun to make light of his plans.

Randy was hysterical with laughter. He began laughing and could not seem to stop. When he was able to catch his breath, he asked Clemis what made him think he was so special that a school teacher would marry him. A man with 11 young'uns. Randy didn't notice the angry look that Clemis was suddenly wearing. He kept on needling Clemis. Randy called Buster from the back to share in the fun. Once Randy told Buster what Clemis had in mind, Buster began to laugh hilariously as well. He thought Clemis' idea was risible.

Buster made an effort to reason with Clemis. He stated that just because Clemis was one of the best vintners in the area; and just because Clemis felt that none of the available women were good enough for him; and just because Clemis was inextricably connected in a bootlegging enterprise, with Sheriff Green as one of his best customers; and just because those teachers were kind to his children, giving the baby girl special attention did not mean one of those teachers was going to stoop to marrying him. "Heck," Buster continued—"those teachers are nice to everyone in Hawk Town. And they treat all of the young students with a special kind of tenderness." Buster told Clemis to wise up! Get a grip! "Don't make a fool of yourself!" With that lecture, Buster walked away and began telling the men in the place about the one-way conversation that had just transpired between Clemis and him. All the men could be heard laughing and whooping at Clemis' ridiculous idea.

Dancie, Buster's cook, overheard the exchange and wondered whether or not the men were taking the joking about Clemis a bit too far. Dancie was a charming young woman who had recently returned to Hawk Town after having spent several years in New York City, where she had worked in one of the dingy factories. Dancie's mother had recently given birth at age 46 and was unable to properly care for the baby alone because she had six other children from a second marriage ranging in ages from 1 to 6 demanding her attention. People of the community called them "stair steps" because their variation in height that coincided with their birth order resembled a staircase. So Dancie was very much needed at home.

During the time she had lived in New York, Dancie had morphed from an innocent country girl to a streetwise city warrior. While living in New York she had earned enough money to not only pay her rent, but she had also been able to send money home to be used to help meet the needs of her younger siblings. She had been able to also set aside a nest egg for a dream she had envisioned. Dancie had long ago developed an entrepreneurial spirit while still living at home, growing up with extremely industrious parents. She had been taught to believe in a theme that a famous author had coined, "Hard work and enterprise would make any person rise to respect and prominence, no matter what." Dancie had been in contact with numerous disingenuous individuals during the two years she had lived in New York City, and she felt she had become acclimated enough to recognize what constituted good business practices. She felt that she knew enough to operate a successful business herself.

Dancie's employment at Buster's was twofold. She served as both cook and accountant. But she was only working there temporarily until she could establish her own place. She wanted to serve a variety of sandwiches—some of which had never been heard of in the South. In the meantime, she intended to remain on good terms with all of Buster's customers and clientele—Clemis included.

When Dancie expressed dismay to Buster about deriding Clemis the way his men had done, telling him she thought the men had taken their rousing a bit too far, Buster responded by telling her that she needed to mind her own business, which did not include analyzing what he and the boys were discussing anytime. So, relative to the discussions held between Buster and the gang who hung out at his place, Dancie vowed to never again offer her opinion. But she felt deep down in her soul that by deriding Clemis, the men were making a humongous mistake.

***

Clemis had been pondering events that might interfere with his plans to marry Miss Madesyn. He knew he had to act hastily because there was a possibility that Mr. Monroe, the Superintendent of Schools, might transfer the two teachers to another town far away from Hawk Town, which would dampen, if not completely extinguish, his chances of capturing Miss Madesyn's heart.

Clemis decided that he was not going to delay the inevitable. He knew Miss Madesyn was going to say, "Yes" when he proposed marriage to her; it was just a matter of his purchasing a ring and asking the question. So on Saturday he was going to drive to Dillington in Old Thumover County and select a ring that he felt was befitting the hand of a school teacher. Clemis was totally unaware that Miss Madesyn had no inclination that he was harboring these affectionate feelings for her. There was no way she could have known that Clemis had plans to use her to fulfill the role of mother for his children—especially his baby girl, Peggy. After all, he surmised, just because Miss Madesyn might be in love with him, he liked her a lot, and was even smitten by her big city mannerisms and her beauty, he was not the kind of man to fall head-over-heels in love with a woman. To everyone who knew him, Clemis was an enigma. Even though his appearance was corpulent, he was handsome in an odd sort of way. He was 6 feet tall; his complexion was smooth and bronzed; his hair was curly, and had once been all black, but now flecks of gray were peppered throughout his curly mane. Clemis had light brown eyes that were always hard to read, as he never had let any emotions surface from what appeared to be his dullard façade. That is, until the two new school teachers came to the Hawk Town community in Granite Point, Kinder County, Xenolina.

In Clemis' mind, women had a place in the family structure, and it was to take care of the husband, the home, and the kids. He had not yet decided whether or not he would even allow Miss Madesyn to continue in her role as school teacher once they were married, but he was thinking that she would have to give it up. There would be enough time for her to manage his home and his kids, but no time to spare for being in school all day.

That just could not be. And once Miss Madesyn became Mrs. Clemis Stapleton, she would not have a say in the matter anyhow.

So on Saturday morning, Clemis woke up early and gave instructions to Cora, his eldest daughter, and Teddy, his eldest son, as to how he wanted the household handled in his absence for four or five hours. He told them that he might be gone most of the day because he really didn't know how long his business would take, but he would be back before nightfall. He told them that by Sunday afternoon, or Monday at the latest, he would have a big, pleasant surprise for the family.

As soon as Clemis' old Chevy pickup truck had left their yard, Teddy and Cora began pondering what Clemis' surprise might be. Teddy was hoping it would be a newer truck, while Cora was hoping for a better stove. She had been hinting how nice it would be to have one of the new electric stoves that she had seen advertised in the newspaper at the general store. It certainly would eliminate her having to start a fire in the wood-burning cook stove they had been using all of her life. A new electric stove would also enable Cora to control the heat temperature and prepare meals much faster. It was no easy task preparing meals for so many people, two, sometimes three times every day. Teddy and Cora decided they would not mention Clemis' plans for a surprise to their siblings. After all, they had no idea what it would be, and there was no need to get the kids all excited over some mysterious gift, if it was a gift, from their daddy.

Clemis arrived at Queenon's Jewelry store 15 minutes after the store opened that Saturday morning. He was greeted by Mrs. Queenon herself, as she generally allowed her salesmen to arrive at the store a couple of hours later on Saturdays. Since it was early and there were no other customers, she was able to give Clemis her undivided attention. When Clemis explained his reason for being there and who his intended bride was, Mrs. Queenon told him she had three rings she thought would be perfect for a young bride-to-be, and she told Clemis he would have to make the choice. The three rings shown to Clemis were exquisite, and Clemis liked all three of them. However, when Mrs. Queenon give Clemis the price of each ring, his earlier excitement and enthusiasm immediately waned. Clemis was a penurious man and he told Mrs. Queenon that he flat out did not care to spend that much money on a ring for a woman. He asked her to show him something less expensive. Mrs. Queenon replaced the three rings and brought three more of lesser quality and beauty for

Clemis to peruse. Clemis chose the tiniest solitaire, simply because it was the cheapest. He made his purchase, thanked Mrs. Queenon, and left the store—all in less than one hour.

After leaving the jewelry store, Clemis drove to the drugstore on Fourth Street for coffee and a sandwich. He was jubilant about his impending plans as he left the drugstore whistling and wondering how excited Miss Madesyn was going to be when he proposed to her. He decided that he could not wait another day. Since this was Saturday, he would dress nicely this evening and go make his wishes known to Miss Madesyn. Because Saturday night was the most popular night for courting in the country, the timing, in Clemis' mind, was perfect.

When Clemis returned home in the afternoon, he was still whistling. Cora was on pins and needles anticipating what surprise her daddy was going to spring on them. But Clemis went about his business around the house and shed, still whistling and not giving away any secrets. Cora could hardly restrain herself. Neither could Teddy. Cora asked Teddy if Clemis had said anything since returning home to him about the big surprise. She received a negative nod from Teddy. They knew they would have to wait until Clemis decided it was time to spring the surprise on them. There was no need to ask him about it.

In the early evening, Clemis had kept to himself and remained outside completing simple, insignificant tasks because he did not want his children to spoil his irrepressible joy. The last thing he did before going inside was cut some roses from the rose bushes that his wife had planted more than 10 years ago before she had passed away. He was really going to impress Miss Madesyn with his thoughtfulness, he was hoping. When he went inside, he took the roses into the kitchen and wrapped them in dampened newspaper. Then he went to his closet and pulled out his Sunday best suit and his only pair of dress shoes. He even selected a white shirt and a colorful necktie. He was going to be dressed to impress the school teachers, and to show them that he owned more than bibbed overalls, chambray or denim shirts, and brogan shoes and cowboy boots.

As Clemis went about polishing himself up for an evening out, Teddy and Cora kept anxiously waiting for him to tell them about his big surprise that had kept them in suspense. When Clemis had finished bathing, shaving, and dressing, he invited Teddy and Cora into his bedroom and asked them to sit for a minute.

Clemis began by asking them not to be upset over what he was about to say. Then he showed them the engagement ring and told them he was going to ask Miss Madesyn for her hand in marriage tonight. He reminded his two oldest children that it had been a little bit more than nine years since their mother had passed. He said Miss Madesyn seems to like him a lot and he knows that she dearly loves Peggy, their youngest sibling. He said Miss Madesyn could take over some of the chores around the house and Cora and her sister Daisy would not have to work as hard as they had been doing for years. When he had finished what he had to say, he asked Teddy and Cora if they had any questions they wanted to ask him before he left.

Teddy and Cora were so astonished, they were speechless. They answered in unison, "No, Daddy." And Clemis said, "Then it's all settled," and he went to the kitchen, picked up the roses, and left. Teddy and Cora were actually stunned by their daddy's revelation. They were both feeling a deep sense of dread. They felt strongly that their father has misinterpreted and misunderstood Miss Madesyn's kindness, and he was about to receive the disappointment of his lifetime. Teddy spoke first and asked Cora what she thought Clemis would do if Miss Madesyn did not accept his proposal—and he felt certain that she would not. Cora was fearing that their daddy was going to be crushed. She said it would be best if all of them went to Sunday School and remained for worship service tomorrow morning to give Clemis time to compose himself. Teddy agreed with that idea and told Cora he would help their younger brothers and sisters to get dressed quietly in order not to disturb Clemis the next morning.

As a rule, all the kids stayed up later than usual on Saturday nights, but this night Teddy and Cora told them they had to be in bed by 9:30 p.m. because everyone was going to have a long day tomorrow at church and would need to be rested. There were a few moans from their siblings, but overall they accepted the instructions without the usual arguments.

By 10 o'clock, everyone was in bed and Clemis had not yet returned home. Teddy and Cora were hoping that perhaps everything had gone well and Clemis and the school teachers were celebrating. But Clemis' experience had been far more humiliating than Teddy and Cora could have imagined.

When Clemis had driven to the teachers' cottage and gotten out of his pickup truck, the two school teachers were surprised to see him. As he came around the truck they could see the roses he had brought. They stepped onto the porch and greeted Clemis with pleasant smiles, even thought they were irritated that he had chosen to drop by on the weekend, and had not mentioned to either of them that he was planning to visit. They also noticed that Clemis was dressed as they had never seen him dress before. He actually looked handsome and distinguished all suited up.

Clemis greeted them as he got closer and said he hoped he was not intruding, but he had some business he needed to discuss with Miss Madesyn if Miss Marie would give them some privacy.

"What sort of business brings you here on a Saturday evening?" Miss Marie inquired. She said if it were in reference to one of his children and some incident that had happened at school, she needed to hear about it, too. Clemis made it clear that that was not the case. He told Miss Marie that his business with Miss Madesyn would not take more than 30 to 45 minutes. So Miss Marie excused herself and returned inside while Clemis and Miss Madesyn sat on the porch swing.

Clemis didn't waste any time. He immediately began to tell Miss Madesyn that he knew she liked him a lot and he had begun to have special feelings toward her. Clemis took the ring from his pocket and told Miss

Madesyn that nothing could make him happier than to have her as his wife.

"Is this some kind of a joke?" she said and began to laugh. She laughed hysterically and so loudly that Marie heard her and come to see what was going on. In between gasps, Madesyn said, "Clemis has proposed to me," and Marie could see the ring Clemis was holding. Then Marie began to laugh uncontrollably. When she could catch her breath, she asked Clemis how he could be so dumb. And that was the question that drove Clemis over the brink of sanity.

Clemis was mortified beyond comprehension. He was too humiliated to speak, and he felt a rage building that was driving him to show these persnickety doyennes of education just whom they were laughing at. He was going to decimate these two women. He was going to show them that he was neither a dullard nor a putz. How dare they laugh at him! Clemis was so enraged that he began to tremble. He took the roses from the table on which he had laid them and slammed them onto the floor. He stormed down the steps, cranked up his old pickup truck, revved the engine, put the gearshift into low gear, mashed the accelerator to the floor, and did a tailspin in the yard, kicking up dirt that flew all over the porch and, in the process, covered the teachers with dirt as well. They were both shocked and in a state of disbelief seeing Clemis' reaction and behavior. Marie said it was a bad omen. She suggested they clean the dirt off the porch quickly and get back into the house and lock up for the night.

***

Clemis had been spurned by Miss Madesyn and derided by Miss Marie, and he was furious and fuming so intensely that he felt as if his pores were sweating fire water from his body. He was trembling and cursing with spit flying from his mouth. He was hot enough to light a fire with his touch, and it occurred to him that a fire was the only way to cover the crime he was contemplating.

In the meanwhile, Clemis was too upset to go home. He was feeling too ashamed to face his children since he had revealed his plans to them and now it all seemed like a bad dream. He asked himself how he could have been so foolish. He decided to drive down to the river and sit for a while. He would wait until everyone in the community was asleep and then he was going to see that those two bitches burned in hell.

Clemis was so angry and distraught that four hours had passed without his having realized it. When his head cleared slightly, he decided it was time to go back to the cottage and carry out what needed to be done. He was sure that by this hour of the night, all the country folks were sound asleep. He cranked up the engine, turned the old pickup truck around, and headed back to the teachers' cottage. He drove with the headlights turned off, and once he reached their yard, he took his shotgun out of the rack, checked to be sure both barrels were loaded, reached in his glove box and got two extra shell for good measure, and headed toward the front door of the cottage. He kicked the door in and the sound of it awakened Miss Marie and she was startled by a noise downstairs. She reached for the flashlight she kept beside her bed, got up, and started down the stairs.

Clemis, although he could not see which one of the sisters it was, pulled the trigger and blasted Miss Marie, who immediately crumpled on the stairs.

Madesyn was awakened by the loud boom and was getting up to see where the noise was coming from when she saw Clemis' silhouette in the door. Before she could react or say anything, Clemis shot her at close range. Needless to say, the gun shot nearly cut her body in half.

Clemis turned and went back down the stairs. He had to step over Miss Marie's body on the way back down.

Clemis left the murder scene and doubled back home and retrieved the two spare cans of gasoline he kept in the shed for his tractor. He gathered some old newspapers that he kept in the shed as fire starter whenever he needed to burn the fields. He took an old hoe handle and some cord and wrapped the cord around the end of the stick of wood to hold the newspaper intact. This would serve as his torch. Clemis put all the items in the bed of his old pickup truck and drove back to the teachers' cottage.

Clemis' behavior was akin to an insane person. In fact, Clemis was so overcome with anger that he had gone temporarily insane. Yet he had the presence of mind to tell himself that even though he had gotten rid of those two highfalutin', skinny, stiff-necked, straight-back bitches who walked around with their smart ass heads in the air all the time, he was not going to prison for killing them. He had showed them that no woman laughed at Clemis without paying a heavy price. Did they think he was going to allow them to walk around peacefully while all the boys at Buster's Place, and some of the ladies in Hawk Town--and children, too--laughed at him? Clemis Stapleton was not going to be the object of people's fun and pity! He had solved that problem.

Clemis was not concerned about anyone hearing the commotion because the cottage was isolated from any nearby neighbors. As a matter of fact, the closest neighbor was almost a mile down the road from the cottage. He went to his pickup truck and took one of the cans of gasoline he had brought along. He went upstairs and poured gasoline all over Madesyn's body. Then, half way down the stairs where Marie had fallen, he dashed the liquid that remained in the can over her.

Clemis went back to his truck and retrieved the second can of fuel. He spread gasoline all over the beautiful antique furniture in the parlor and all through the kitchen. He then went outside and lit fire to the newspaper he had attached to the old broken hoe handle to create his makeshift torch. After he lit the torch, he threw it into the kitchen and backed away quickly so as not to catch fire himself. He stood outside as if he were in a trance and watched the fire engulf the stately old cottage. He felt certain that his crime would be smothered in the ashes.

After he was confident that there was no evidence left around that could link the crime to him, he returned home, gathered a few clothes, and threw them into an old suitcase he pulled from his nearly empty closet. He took the ring that he had grudgingly purchased for Miss

Madesyn out of his pocket, got a pencil from the Mason jar that was kept in the kitchen, took a sheet of paper from one of his kid's notebook that was lying on their study table in the corner of the room, and wrote a note to Teddy.

Clemis told his son that he wanted him to have the engagement ring so that he could give it to Joyce. Clemis said he knew that Teddy wanted to marry Joyce, but had not given her a ring yet—perhaps because he felt he could not afford one at this time. He went to the cupboard and took the receipt from Queenon's and stated in the note that if Teddy did not like the ring, he could return it and choose one to his liking. He further stated in the note that he had to go away and might be gone for a long time. He told Teddy that he was leaving the key in the pickup truck because he knew Teddy would need it for transporting the children and he would also need the truck for truck farming. Lastly, he told Teddy that he might understand everything in a day or two. But in the meantime, Teddy must burn the note and never breathe a word of its contents to anyone, including his sister, Cora. And again he apologized for having to leave, but he said he knew that Teddy and Cora would take good care of the family.

Clemis then took the note, the ring, and the receipt, and tiptoed into the boys' bedroom and placed everything on the dresser beside Teddy's bed. He peeped into the girls' bedroom and knew that this would probably be the last time he would ever see them. Then he picked up the old suitcase he had left standing at the door, and walked away from his family and his crime.

***

Peggy was awake when Clemis returned home. She heard his pickup truck when he pulled into the driveway and parked back at the shed. She didn't know for certain what he was doing, but assumed that Clemis and the sheriff were about to make one of their late night business deals. However, she heard Clemis rumbling about but Zack Green's cruiser never showed up. It wasn't long before she heard Clemis' truck leave again. Peggy wondered, first of all, why he had come back home so late, and secondly, why he was leaving again. Not hearing anything further, she dozed off to sleep.

Peggy, being an insomniac and light sleeper, would wake up at the sound of the proverbial pin falling. An hour later, she was awakened this time by the sound of the old pickup truck coming back into the yard. She saw Clemis, with urgency, park in his usual spot, get out, close the truck door quietly, and enter the house. She heard Clemis enter his bedroom. Approximately 10 minutes later, she saw the door open to the bedroom where she was supposed to be sleeping—but she wasn't—with her sisters, and she could see Clemis' silhouette as he stood in the doorway briefly. He closed the door quietly and then she heard him stealthily creep into the boys' room. In another few minutes she heard Clemis go back to the kitchen, and then he left the house through the back door. Peggy tiptoed to the window and peeped out to see if Clemis was going out to the shed. When she spotted him, she noticed he had in his hand the old suitcase that he always kept in his closet.

"What in the world is he doing?" she wondered. Then she saw Clemis walk around the side of the house and go straightaway out of the yard onto Hawk Town Road, headed in the direction of Highway 102. Peggy suddenly had an uncomfortable feeling and she lay awake until dawn, her usual time for getting up and starting her day.

Peggy noticed that the door to Clemis' bedroom was closed when they left for Sunday School and Worship Service, and she knew he was not in his room. From the time she had seen Clemis leave with the old piece of luggage until she got up this morning, Clemis had not returned. She knew this because she never went back to sleep after Clemis left home with the old suitcase in his hand.

Peggy could not concentrate on the lesson that Sunday because she kept thinking about Clemis. And all during worship service she was restless. She could hardly wait until they returned home because she wanted to know if her daddy was back. And when the Stapleton family returned home that afternoon, she could see that Clemis wasn't there. No one else in the family seemed to notice that Clemis had not been seen all day. Teddy didn't mention him and neither did Cora or Daisy. Everyone was doing what they usually did on Sundays after church and acting as if everything was OK. But deep down inside, Peggy had a hollow feeling. But she was not going to ask questions about her daddy until someone else mentioned him first.

***

In Hawk Town, as in most country communities, on Sunday morning nearly every living soul attended Sunday School and church. The exception was the men who frequented Buster's Place and the harlots living at Miss Circe's Place. But every so often, some of the church ladies would drag their sinful husbands along with them if there was a special program taking place. And although Miss Circe was a regular churchgoer and strong financial supporter of Mt. Mercy Church, she wouldn't dare allow those girls of hers to set a foot inside the church. Why, the snooty ladies of Hawk Town would have a conniption if that happened.

This Sunday morning, when everyone had arrived and was seated in their respective Sunday School classes, everyone noticed that Miss Marie and Miss Madesyn were not in the sanctuary. That was unusual because those two ladies were the most punctual of all the members. After another five minutes had passed, Rev. Herman asked if anyone had seen or heard from the two school teachers this morning. No one had. So, the congregation went ahead with devotion and when it was over, the lessons began.

At the end of Sunday School classes, there was still no sign of the school teachers. Rev. Herman said perhaps one of them, or both of them, wasn't feeling well this morning and they were not present for that reason. He said that following worship service this afternoon, he would go by and check on the ladies and see if there was anything they needed. And then he called the service to order.

When worship service ended, and the usual pleasantries that followed the closing of another wonderful and uplifting sermon that had been delivered by Rev. Herman, he retired to the pastor's study, put away his Bible, and began collecting his personal items and keys to his car. He asked First Lady Herman to get a ride home with her brother, Simeon, and told her he would be home soon after he had checked on Miss Marie and Miss Madesyn to satisfy himself that they were OK.

On the drive to the cottage, Rev. Herman could not help but notice what a bright and beautiful day the Good Lord had given them this Sunday. He had preached about the goodness of the Lord and how the Sabbath Day should be a day of rest. Today, he had taken his sermon from the book of Deuteronomy and emphasized Chapter 5, verses 13 and 14: "Six days thou shall labor and do all thy work. But the seventh day is the Sabbath of the Lord thy God; in it thou shall not do any work; thou nor thy son, nor thy daughter, nor thy manservant, nor thy maidservant, nor thine ox, nor thine ass, nor any of thy cattle, nor thy stranger that is within thy gates; that thy manservant and thy maidservant may rest as well as thou."

Rev. Herman felt it was especially important to focus on this particular passage in the Bible at the present time because some of the newcomers to the area did not seem to understand that around these parts everyone knew that no one was supposed to work on Sunday. Since a number of new faces were interspersed throughout the congregation today, he hoped that they would take his message to heart and adhere to the common practices of the local folks.

When Rev. Herman came out of the fog of thoughts and snapped back to reality, he was taken aback by the sight that appeared before him. In the distance he could see wood smoldering, and where the teachers' cottage once stood so stately and elegantly, there lay only cinders, burned-out rafters, and lots of ashes. The few things that were recognizable from what once was a cottage were the brick steps leading to the front porch, tin from what was once a roof, metal frame from what was once beds, the pump and sink in what was once a kitchen, the chimney, and stone pilings that supported the weight of the cottage itself. Rev. Herman was horrified! He opened his car door and got out. There was no sign of life around the grounds of what once was a cottage. For a few minutes Rev. Herman was so stupefied he felt numb. He could not imagine what had caused such a tragedy, and mentally he could not consider the possibility that both teachers had lost their lives in a fire with no one around to help them. Rev. Herman released a loud squall and fell to his knees and began to pray. He prayed for strength to get up and seek help; he prayed that the two teachers had not been victims in the fire; and, most of all, he prayed that the scene he was witnessing had not been caused by any man-made malicious actions. And as soon as Rev. Herman regained his composure, he got back into his car, turned it around, and sped away from the scene.

The floozies were relaxing on Miss Circe's front porch enjoying a leisurely Sunday afternoon because business was always slow after church on Sundays. They would not begin to receive clients until nightfall. They took notice of Rev. Herman's vehicle speeding past their place of business because Rev. Herman was never known to speed, even when he was in a hurry. So, something must have been terribly wrong. They were thinking that whatever it was had happened at church, so Lola rushed inside and asked Miss Circe, who had attended worship service, if anything unusual had happened at Mt. Mercy today. Miss Circe let her know that nothing out of the ordinary had occurred, and she was curious to know why Lola had asked the question. When Lola explained how Rev. Herman had driven past the house at a high rate of speed, Miss Circe, too, felt that action in itself portended trouble.

Miss Circe told her wanton bunch that she was going to ride out to the Granite Point crossroads where the sheriff had a department annex office, and see if Zack Green had any news on why Rev. Herman's driving was totally uncharacteristic today. On the drive there, she met Zack Green and two of his deputies, with Rev. Herman in tow, driving at a high rate of speed with their blue lights flashing and sirens screaming. When they had passed her, Miss Circe asked her driver to turn around and follow them. They turned off Highway 102 and back onto Hawk Town Road, and a mile and a quarter later, turned left onto Grateful Road. The cottage, or what was left of it, was at the end of Grateful Road.

As soon as the burned-out house came into view, Miss Circe cried out, "Oh, my God! What in the world has happened here?" Before the driver brought the car to a complete stop, Miss Circe had jumped out of the vehicle and went running behind the sheriff, his two deputies, and Rev. Herman. Zack Green turned around and told Rev. Herman and Miss Circe that they could not come any further. He explained that the area had to be secured for the fire investigators. As he looked at the scene again and noticed what appeared to be a body on the metal bed frame that was still visible from under the fallen tin roof, he instructed one of his deputies to get on the radio and call the coroner. Then he said absent mindedly, "What a mess!"

This situation was going to require an intensive investigation to try and determine both the cause of the fire and the cause of death of the two victims. Zack was assuming that the other twin bed frame that was covered completely by the fallen tin roof held the body of the other victim. And the automatic assumption was that the two victims were the two school teachers.

While the sheriff was assessing the scene and one deputy, as instructed, was attempting to radio the coroner, the second deputy was also making an assessment. But instead of looking at the burned-out building, he was studying the tire tracks. He could see where someone had made a tailspin in the yard and had flung dirt in the direction of the house. He noticed tire tracks leaving the yard, and he noticed tire tracks with the same treads returning to the yard. He knew that, because where one set of tracks crossed the other set, the directions were different and pointing in a manner that let him know which set of tire prints was going out and which set of tire prints was coming into the yard.

The deputy pointed out his observation to the sheriff and Zack then instructed the deputy to call in his two top investigators. He said to tell them what he had observed, and ask them to bring all equipment at their disposal that will help solve this mystery.

When the community folks got word that the two school teachers had been killed in a house fire, everyone was sad—especially all of the school kids because Miss Marie and Miss Madesyn were endeared to them.

At the Stapleton home, however, as the school-age children were quiet and sad, Teddy was having a serious silent conversation with himself. He was thinking about the note Clemis had left him that no one else knew about, and the ring Clemis had told him he could have to give to Joyce. He was remembering that his sister, Cora, had seen the ring because Clemis had shown it to both of them. And he was thinking that he needed to take the receipt and go to Queenon's and exchange the ring for a new one for Joyce as soon as possible before Cora stumbled across it in his bureau drawer. He would go to Dillington tomorrow. If anyone at the jewelry store began asking questions about why he was making the exchange, he would say his daddy felt that he could make a better selection, and had given him extra money to upgrade to a better choice of ring.

Teddy was wondering if Clemis could be responsible for what had happened to the two school teachers and their cottage. And, most of all, he was wondering where Clemis had gone. It was as if he had vanished into thin air. But thus far, amid all of the excitement, none of the kids had asked about Clemis. And he was pondering what he should tell them when they did ask—because sooner or later, before the day was over, they were going to ask.

Cora, subdued herself, was noticing how self-engrossed Teddy appeared to be. She was thinking that he was worried about Clemis just like she was. She was also thinking that she needed to ask Teddy to go outside so that they could talk privately. So, she got Teddy's attention and motioned for him to go outside. She and Teddy went behind the shed where there was a wooden bench, and they both sat silently for a while.

Cora broke the silence by asking Teddy, "What do you think has happened to Daddy? It is so unlike him to disappear for so many hours and not let us know where he was going."

Both Teddy and Cora knew that the last place Clemis was headed was to the teachers' cottage to propose to Miss Madesyn. Teddy spoke up and said, "I don't think we should tell anyone that Daddy was going to that cottage. We don't even know if he went there. Maybe he lost his nerve about proposing to Miss Madesyn."

Cora replied, "Maybe. But why hasn't he come home? And if he doesn't show up soon, what are we going to tell the kids? After all, his truck is here at the house."

Teddy said, "Let's tell them that maybe he went for a walk, or decided to go hunt some squirrels."

"On Sunday!" Cora exclaimed. "No one goes hunting on Sunday!" Then Teddy said, "Well, let's just tell them that we don't know, because we really don't. And let's just say he will probably be back soon." Then as an afterthought, he said, "Maybe he caught a ride with someone and is over at Buster's Place."

Cora asked Teddy to go check at Buster's if Clemis was not back soon because it was getting late and would be dark in several hours. Teddy said he would.

***

Back at the scene of the fire, while there was still some daylight the investigators were working while it was still bright enough to glean as much as possible about what might have caused this tragedy while there was still some daylight. They had gotten some good clean casts of the tire tracks, and tomorrow they were planning to begin looking for matches to what they had collected.

Monday morning, bright and early, the two detectives began combing Hawk Town searching for a match to the tire print casts they had in their possession. Their first stop was the construction site where the new school was being built. They looked meticulously at every tire on every vehicle at that location. After searching for two full hours, they had not found a match.

The investigators decided that the next location they were most likely to find a match would be where Highway 102 crossed the river because that's where the Northeast Cape Dread new river bridge was under construction. For some reason the investigating detectives felt that, in all likelihood, when they found tires that matched the casts, they would belong to one of the transient construction workers, because they did not believe that a member of the local community could be that cold and callous toward those two nice school teachers. And the most likely motive would have been robbery, which didn't make much sense because everybody knew that school teachers were poorly paid and could barely make ends meet. It was not a profession that one chose for money, but for the love of helping promote the growth and development of children. All the vehicles they examined at the river bridge construction site yielded the same results. No match!

By the time the detectives had completed conducting the search at the river bridge construction site, it was pretty close to lunchtime. The investigators knew that Buster's Place was where locals commonly frequented for some of Miss Dancie's good food at lunchtime. So on a hunch, they decided to order sandwiches and sodas at Buster's Place, and hang around to check out tires on the sly of patrons coming in for a bite. They hung out at Buster's for an hour, and left sooner than they had planned because it was noticeably clear that their presence at the joint made everyone uncomfortable—this is, except Miss Dancie, of course. She was enjoying the fact that they were there because even though the guys appeared somewhat distressed having the investigators around, more and more customers were dropping in out of curiosity, but they were also ordering lunch, even if it was to take it out. In any case, the situation, as it was playing out, was very good for business.

When the two detectives left Buster's Place having been unsuccessful in their cursory search one more time, they decided that the best recourse to take now would be to visit door-to-door and check the tires at every individual residence. This was going to be a time-consuming and daunting task, but they could see no other way to ensure that every vehicle had had its tires carefully checked for a match to the tire casts they had collected from the school teachers' yard. For now, they would return to department headquarters and begin a fresh start tomorrow morning.

Tuesday morning could not have started out more beautifully. A bright sun rose and lit up a cloudless blue sky. Community folks were working in fields early in a race against nothing in particular, but it was simply the perfunctory way country folks ordered their lifestyle. The two investigators were hopeful that this day would yield some positive results for their efforts.

On the drive from Marigold, location of the sheriff department's headquarters, the investigators decided that if there were vehicles parked at the edge of fields as they entered Hawk Town, they would check those vehicles first. And, sure enough, there were one and two vehicles, respectively, parked at the first two fields they approached. They had no luck at the first field, but at their stop at the second field, they had a eureka moment.

The pickup truck owned by Clemis Stapleton was parked at the end of the Stapleton's fields. As the two men exited their vehicle to speak to Teddy Stapleton, who was just climbing onto Clemis' old tractor, they got an up-close look at the truck's tires. They did not let Teddy know what they were looking for specifically, but told him they were investigating the deaths of the two school teachers, and were wondering if he or his daddy or any members of his family had noticed anything unusual in the community Saturday, especially Saturday evening. Teddy said they had not. The investigators asked Teddy to contact them if he or any member of his family thought of anything, and they left with him one of their cards on which the sheriff department's number was printed.

After having found the tires that were the source of the tracks at the cottage where the two school teachers had died in a fire, the detectives returned to headquarters to discuss their findings with the sheriff. They needed instructions coming directly from him as to how he would like to proceed with the investigation. All three of them felt strongly that Teddy Stapleton didn't have a clue about the trail of evidence that had been left at what the investigators considered a potential crime scene. They would know for certain if it were so once John Riverbank completed autopsies on what was left of the two bodies.

It had to be an act of divine intervention that the two bodies had not been completely decimated in the fire. Fortunately for the coroner, the upper bodies were intact, with the major burns on the extremities. He would be able to check both pairs of lungs for smoke inhalation, which would let him know whether or not that was the cause of death. He needed to know that because both bodies had gunshot wounds that could have killed the victims, or they could have been shot after having died from the poisonous gases from smoke prior to having been shot.

John needed to begin these two autopsies immediately, giving them first priority over other cases that were in need of his attention. The two school teachers were not Hawk Town natives—they weren't even natives of Xenolina; they were born and raised in Washington, D.C. It had been an agonizing experience for Zack Green having to deliver the news to the two school teachers' parents that their only two children had died in a fire. It was a dreadful, heartrending situation, but they needed to have their daughters' bodies returned to Washington as soon as possible so that arrangements could be made for a funeral service. Mr. and Mrs. Moore had made a rational decision to have their daughters' bodies cremated once they were in the possession of their local undertaker, because there was little reason to have bodies that had been burned beyond recognition eulogized in caskets.

After a thorough operation had been completed on both bodies and the organs had been set out before him and analyzed, John could see that both victims had died as a result of gunshots to their bodies. Their lungs were clear, which meant they were dead long before the fire started. The coroner needed to pass along his findings to the sheriff expediently because somebody had killed these two wonderful human beings, and they needed to be caught and prosecuted to the fullest extent of the law. So the coroner took a break from his immediate tasks and went forthwith to the sheriff's department. He laid out his findings before the sheriff and the two detectives handling the case, and returned to his office.

With the information the coroner had delivered to them, the sheriff instructed the detectives to go and invite Teddy Stapleton to come to the station for questioning. If Teddy refused, they were to let him know that he could be arrested on suspicion of murder.

When the detectives returned to Hawk Town, Teddy was no longer in the field. He had finished the work there yesterday and had taken the tractor back to the shed at the Stapleton property. And that's where they found him, cleaning the disks he had used to plow the fields. The detectives told Teddy they needed to ask him some questions, and wondered if he would be willing to come to the sheriff's department in Marigold, which was nine miles away. Teddy let them know immediately that he was willing to do that. He would drive there as soon as he changed clothes because he had gotten dirty in the field.

During the drive to Marigold, Teddy was dealing with the anguish of having to tell about his daddy's escapade. He felt that must be the reason they wanted to interview him because he was not guilty of any illegal activity—misdemeanor or felony—and to his knowledge, no one else in the family had engaged in any unacceptable activities or participated in anything illegal. It had to be Clemis they had questions about. Teddy would be truthful relative to everything they asked. After all, he was in charge of the family now, and he could not afford to invite trouble from any angle, especially from lying to law enforcement officers.

Within 30 minutes after the detectives had returned to Marigold, Teddy came into the station and asked to see Sheriff Green and the detectives investigating the deaths of the two school teachers. They were waiting for him in the interview room.

After introductions were made, Zack Green explained the purpose of this interview. The first question they asked Teddy was had he driven to the teachers' cottage over the weekend. Teddy let them know he had not. Then they asked Teddy had anyone else driven the pickup truck over the weekend, whereby Teddy told the investigators that Clemis was the only one who had use of the pickup during the past weekend. The sheriff asked Teddy where was Clemis because he had been looking for him but had been unable to locate him anywhere around Granite Point. Teddy responded by saying he did not know. So, the sheriff asked Teddy when was the last time he had seen Clemis, and Teddy said he saw Clemis Saturday evening, but not since then.

Now, one of the detectives began to interrogate Teddy. He told Teddy that if he knew anything that could help them in their investigation, he needed to speak up while he had this opportunity to do so.

Otherwise, he could be charged with harboring a fugitive, if that was the case, or impeding an investigation.

Teddy began to feel uneasy. He was thinking about the note his daddy had left on the dresser, as well as the ring. He was also thinking that Mrs. Queenon might remember Clemis coming into the jewelry store once she read about his disappearance in the newspaper, should a story surface about Clemis. Teddy contemplated all possibilities for a few minutes while the sheriff and the detectives waited patiently for him to respond.

As much as Teddy hated to betray his daddy, he decided that the best thing to do was to tell these investigators everything that he knew, because he would never believe that Clemis had caused the death of those two school teachers. Clemis wanted to marry Miss Madesyn, so in Teddy's mind, Clemis would never have harmed her.

Teddy looked the detectives in the eye and began to tell what he knew. He told them that Clemis had planned to ask Miss Madesyn to marry him. Although the detectives and the sheriff were somewhat shocked to hear this, they did not interrupt. Teddy went on to say that Clemis had purchased an engagement ring from

Queenon's Jewelry Store Saturday morning and when he left home at first dark, around 7 o'clock Saturday evening, he was headed to the teachers' cottage. Teddy said no one in the family had seen Clemis since then. He told them about the note and the ring that Clemis had left for him, and that was everything in a nutshell.

Teddy had expressed himself convincingly. The story he had divulged to the three men was believable. They reasoned that Teddy would have no need to fabricate a tale like the one he had just told them. So, they excused themselves and stepped outside the interview room briefly and decided to let Teddy return to his family.

When they re-entered the room, Teddy had not moved from the seat where they had left him. Zack Green told Teddy he was free to go. He told Teddy that if he, or any member of his family, heard from Clemis, they were to immediately notify the sheriff or either one of the detectives handling the case. The sheriff also told Teddy that the tires on Clemis' pickup truck were evidence in this case. He instructed Teddy to drive the truck around back to the department's garage and one of the technicians would remove the tires from the pickup and exchange them with a new set of tires. He said it should only take about 45 minutes. Teddy told the sheriff that was not a problem, and when he left them, he exited the building and drove around to the garage where two technicians were waiting to remove Teddy's tires and replace them with a different set. It took the approximately 45 minutes to make the switch.

On the return trip home, Teddy decided that he needed to share what had transpired at the sheriff's department with his oldest sister, Cora. After all, she knew as much as he did about the situation with Clemis. He felt that he and Cora should not say anything to their younger siblings about his having been interviewed by the sheriff because it would be too upsetting for them—especially in the wake of Clemis' absence.

Along the drive, Teddy also thought about Joyce. He loved her and did not want to keep any secrets from her. He thought it might be a betrayal if he was not completely open and honest with her. With all the gossip he felt would spread through Hawk Town about Clemis' possible involvement, and may even be a potential suspect in the school teachers' demise, he needed to make Joyce aware of his visit to the sheriff's department and what it entailed, before someone else mentioned it to her first. He would stop by Miss Circe's and ask to speak to Joyce now since he had to pass there on his way home.

When Teddy arrived at Miss Circe's, Joyce was in the kitchen preparing lunch. One of the floozies spotted Teddy as soon as he was pulling into the driveway and went back to let Joyce know he was here. Joyce stopped in the middle of making a sandwich and went to greet Teddy on the front porch. Teddy asked to speak to her privately for a moment, so the two harlots who were sitting on the porch got up and went into the house, leaving Joyce and Teddy alone.

Teddy shared his experience with the sheriff and told Joyce he did not believe his daddy was capable of committing such a horrendous crime, but because he had been contacted and questioned by two detectives and the sheriff himself, he needed to let her know before someone else distorted and exaggerated the reason for his appearance in Marigold this morning.

Joyce, knowing Teddy, was convinced that he had done nothing wrong, and she said as much to him. She asked him not to worry and told him that she would be there for him no matter what. She asked if there was anything she could do at the moment, and Teddy said, "Just don't stop loving me." She responded by reaching out and kissing him hungrily, and when they broke away from each other, she told him there was not a chance of that ever happening. Then Teddy got up to leave and Joyce walked with him to his truck.

When Teddy arrived home, Cora was in the kitchen preparing lunch for all the kids. Teddy told her that after the kids had been served lunch, he needed to discuss something with her. So she hurriedly finished and after Cora had taken care of all their siblings, she and Teddy walked to the wooden bench behind the shed and sat down. Teddy repeated to her the exact account he had given to Joyce approximately 30 minutes earlier. Cora agreed that their younger brothers and sisters should not be entangled in something they were too young to comprehend. So, that was settled and Teddy and Cora returned to finish their chores.

***

When Clemis stole away from Hawk Town in the wee hours of the morning that he had murdered the two school teachers and burned the cottage they were renting, he assumed he had covered his tracks so well that no one would be able to link him to the crime—not even John Riverbank, as smart as he was known to be. As for Zack Green—Zack was his friend and partner in the crime of bootlegging, so to speak. Plus, Zack was no angel himself. Everyone knew about his adulterous nature and the fact that the boy, Casper, was his son. So, Clemis wasn't worried about being tracked down by Zack, even if he were able to figure out what had happened to the teachers and their cottage. It was doubtful in Clemis' mind that Zack would be smart enough to put the puzzle pieces together because his light bulb never burned any brighter than 40 watts.

Under the cover of darkness, Clemis stole away and made it to the home of a trucker whom he knew would be traveling to the market in Silverboro. Raymond Ross, owner of Ross' Fresh Produce, usually left home at 5 o'clock every weekday morning on his way to the market in Silverboro, where he sold the vegetables that he had grown. He was known to have one of the largest farms in northern Kinder County, and had earned a reputation over the years for offering fair prices for the best fruits and vegetables money could buy.

Clemis knew that oftentimes Raymond made the trip to Silverboro early on Sunday mornings if he had harvested any crops on Saturday. He always prided himself in having fresh produce. So, Clemis was hoping this was one of those Sunday mornings that Raymond would be headed north. Clemis made it to Highway 711 in record time on foot because he was running on adrenaline, and reaching his destination was a matter of life or death. He made it to Raymond's truck where it was parked at the edge of the yard and lifted the canvas cover to see if the truck was loaded for the market. Sure enough, it was. Clemis relaxed a bit for the first time since committing the heinous crime back in Hawk Town. He decided to sit in the truck and wait. Clemis had not slept since Friday night, so he dozed off moments after he had climbed into the truck's cab.

Clemis was awakened at 4:45 when Raymond came outside to warm the truck's engine before beginning his journey to Silverboro. Both men were startled seeing each other. Raymond had not expected to find anyone in his truck, and Clemis was startled because he was awakened suddenly—not realizing he had fallen asleep. Clemis apologized to Raymond, and told him he needed a ride to Silverboro. He explained that he had gotten word that his sister, who lives in New York City, was gravely ill, and he needed to catch the Greyhound bus in order to get to her as quickly as possible. Raymond said he would be happy to give Clemis a lift, and he hoped that Clemis would find his sister in better health when he reached her.

When the truck's engine had warmed enough, Raymond and Clemis started on their way. Initially, Raymond did most, if not all, of the talking—telling

Clemis about his crops and the fact that this year had been one of his most successful years. He told Clemis about his oldest son who had recently joined the U.S. Army and was now stationed at Fort Gordon, Ga., in basic training. Raymond said he didn't know where his son would be shipped out to when his basic training was complete, but he was hoping he would be sent to Fort Bragg, N.C., so that the family could visit him periodically, or his son could come home for a visit some weekends. But, he said, it was unlikely that would happen because usually, following basic training, the guys were sent far away from home.

Raymond noticed that Clemis was silent and mostly unresponsive to his effort for a two-way conversation. So, he told Clemis that he understood that he was worried about his sister, and he would be praying that everything would be alright. Clemis nodded, but still did not speak, so Raymond turned on the radio and tuned in to a Gospel station. They rode the rest of the trip in silence.

When Raymond reached the town of Silverboro, he took Clemis straight to the bus terminal and wished him godspeed. Clemis offered Raymond a $5 bill, which Raymond refused to accept. Clemis thanked him and disappeared into the bus terminal. It would be several weeks before Raymond would hear rumors about what Clemis was alleged to have done.

When Clemis checked with the ticket agent, the bus bound for New York would be departing at 8 o'clock, giving Clemis a two-hour delay at the station. Clemis was nervous and did not care to be sitting inside the bus terminal for several hours because by this time someone might have discovered what he had done back in Hawk Town. He was hoping that the country folks in his community were, as was customary, sleeping late on Sunday morning and still oblivious to their surroundings. Clemis would not be able to relax a bit more until he was on the bus leaving this town.

At 8 o'clock sharp, the call came over the intercom for everyone with tickets to New York to get onboard. Clemis, who had been hanging outside, was the third person in line. Once on the bus he took the seat at the very back. He was hoping no one else would choose that seat because it stretched across the entire width of the bus, and he was planning to lie down and extend his legs as if he were in his bed. He was so tired.

***

When Raymond Ross returned home Sunday evening from his trip to the Farmers' Market in

Silverboro, he was exhausted. He told his wife that he was thinking about taking the produce they harvested tomorrow south to Marigold and Granite Point to save himself from the two-hour long drive to Silverboro. He would sell locally for two days and then return to Silverboro on Wednesday. By that time he should feel rested and ready to take the long drive again.

On Monday afternoon, Raymond and his two teenage sons drove the fresh produce that had just been harvested that morning to the Farmers' Market in Marigold. Business was good there also. Produce was being purchased as quickly as Raymond's son could set it out for eager customers. Corn was being racked up by the bushel, as were green beans, baby lima beans, and cow peas. Raymond was selling his squash, zucchini, potatoes, cabbage, collards, and peppers as fast as they could be unloaded from his refrigerated truck. He was glad his sons, ages 14 and 16, had come along on this trip. They were jewels in a crunch.

Later on, when customers were coming to them more sporadically, Raymond told his sons to walk down to the drugstore and bring him back an ice cold Pepsi and a honey bun. When the two young masters returned, they asked Raymond the name of the man

Raymond told them he had given a ride to Silverboro Sunday morning.

"His name is Clemis Stapleton," Raymond told his sons. The two boys gave each other a baffling look, and then turned to face their daddy. "What's the matter?" Raymond wanted to know. Then his sons told him that down at the drugstore people were gossiping about a man named Clemis Stapleton, and they were saying that the sheriff had been looking for him.

"Did they say why?" Raymond asked.

"No, not that we could hear," his 14-year-old son replied.

Raymond said, "Well, I'll be!" I thought he was acting a little bit too nervous about his sister being real sick. It must be something else, and I am going to try and find out what it is. Don't you boys mention anything I told you about giving that man a ride yesterday! Do you understand?"

"Yes, sir!" they replied in unison.

When all was settled at the Ross residence Monday night—dinner had been served, the kitchen had been cleaned, the boys settled in their room playing games and joshing around—Raymond told his wife what their sons relayed to him earlier that afternoon when they had returned from the drugstore in Marigold. Raymond told his wife that he was deeply troubled over the fact that he might have unknowingly aided a fugitive from justice—that is, if Clemis had done anything wrong. His wife said to Raymond that perhaps the sheriff was looking for Clemis for some other reason because practically everyone knew about their shady relationship. Raymond said, "But if he has committed a crime, I could be in a lot of trouble if the authorities learned that I had given Clemis a lift and thought I had been aware of the fact that Clemis was on the run." He said that tomorrow he would take their produce to the Granite Point crossroads, sell vegetables there, and see if he could find out more details about why the sheriff was asking questions about Clemis.

On Tuesday, when Raymond Ross set out his fruit and vegetable display in Granite Point, it was one of those glorious sunny mornings that energized country folks to get out and about early to complete chores, run errands, or head to the beach for a day of fun. For vendors at the crossroads, a morning such as this was good for business. Tourists headed to Bottomsail Beach would stop by the produce stands and tents to make purchases knowing that the farm produce was fresh picked. For some unexplained reason, they were delighted by this notion, as opposed to making a trip to the grocery store or supermarket to acquire the same essential produce.

Raymond enjoyed chatting with both tourists and local folks who would drop by to peruse and purchase whatever produce he happened to be selling on a given day. Today, Raymond was especially interested in conversing with any resident of Granite Point and surrounding hamlets because he wanted to find out what was being whispered about Clemis Stapleton's disappearance. More importantly, he wanted to know if there was any possibility that he, himself, might be in trouble because he had given Clemis a lift out of town.

Business was good this morning with folks coming and going, but so far Raymond had not been able to strike up the right conversation to discover what he was longing to know. By lunchtime Raymond was even more anxious and had given up on hearing the buzz about Clemis from his customers because everyone who stopped by this morning seemed to be in a hurry and not very chatty. Maybe it was the heat or simply the fact that the moon would be full tonight. As Raymond was pondering the situation and trying to decide if there was another way for him to get the skinny on Clemis, he saw Zack Green going into the modular building that served as the sheriff department's annex, and to alleviate his anxiety, Raymond decided on the spot to go talk to Zack Green if the sheriff had a few minutes to spare. Raymond asked his 16-year-old son to handle the customers for a few minutes while he had a word with the sheriff.

Raymond left the produce stand and walked the short distance to the annex. When he entered the facility, he was greeted pleasantly by a female deputy who asked if Raymond needed any help. Raymond told her he needed to see the sheriff for a few minutes if he was available. The deputy asked Raymond to give her a moment to check, and she did.

While Raymond was waiting, the sheriff opened his office door and invited Raymond to come in. In an affable tone the sheriff said, "Good morning. What can I do for you, Mr. Ross? How's business?"

"Howdy, sheriff. Business is real good right now, thank you."

Then Raymond told the sheriff that he had come to see him to find out a bit of information. He said he had heard that the sheriff was looking for Clemis Stapleton. Raymond further stated that he did not know if Clemis was in trouble, and he wasn't asking because it was none of his business. But there was something he needed to get off of his chest about Clemis because he did not want to be in any trouble.

Then Raymond continued by giving the sheriff the details of his having given Clemis a ride to Silverboro early Sunday morning. He related the fact that Clemis told him he needed to catch the Greyhound bus to New York to see his sister who was gravely ill. Raymond told the sheriff that he dropped Clemis at the Silverboro bus terminal before 8 o'clock Sunday morning, but he did not know if Clemis caught the bus to New York because he did not wait around to see.

The sheriff thanked Raymond for sharing this information with him. He said it was most helpful and would save him and his men a lot of time and energy. He assured Raymond that he had done the right thing by coming to him, and he was not in any trouble because when he gave Clemis a ride, he had no idea that Clemis was on the run.

Raymond then said he needed to get back to his produce stand, and he bid the sheriff good day.

After Raymond left, Zack Green instructed his administrative officer at the annex to notify his detectives on the Stapleton case that they need not waste any more time looking for Clemis in local communities. Clemis had flown the coop.

When the sheriff shared with the detectives investigating the case what he had gleaned from Raymond regarding Clemis and the murder of the two school teachers, he told them he was leaning toward questioning Teddy for further details on his daddy's whereabouts. The investigators could question Teddy again to ascertain the name and address of the aunt in New York whom Clemis told Raymond Ross he was going to visit. If that turned out to be a false lead, they would have no idea where to begin looking for Clemis. The only thing Zack's department could do was share the information on Clemis being a fugitive from justice with other jurisdictions and hope Clemis would make some mistakes and get caught.

The sheriff knew his department had neither the manpower nor financial resources to go traipsing all across the nation, specifically up and down the East Coast in pursuit of Clemis Stapleton. And after all, the charge against Clemis was murder. Since there were no statute of limitations on murder, Zack Green felt he could wait Clemis out. He felt that Clemis would return to Hawk Town sooner or later. Clemis was a country boy and Zack doubted he could survive very long in the city—

especially a city as large as New York—if that's where he went. So in the sheriff's manner of thinking, this was a case whose final resting place would be the cold case files—for now. But tomorrow maybe the investigators would get lucky when they questioned Teddy Stapleton. Perhaps he would provide information to put them on the right path.

The following day when Teddy was questioned, he told the investigators that Clemis did not have any living sisters and, as far as he knew, Clemis didn't know anyone in New York. Like the sheriff, Teddy could not believe Clemis could survive in a city, and it was highly unlikely that he would flee to one. In essence, the detectives believed Teddy and agreed. With no other leads, this case was already running cold.

PART II

In the small Kinder County town of Anderson, approximately 25 miles from Hawk Town, Hugh Manson, one of the wealthiest men in Kinder County, was plotting to kill his wife, Elizabeth. While he was tormented over the idea, because Elizabeth had always been the near- perfect wife, Hugh had fallen in love with a young not-too-fresh maiden, and was smitten to the point of no return. He simply had to have Agatha all to himself or he would rather be dead without her. And Hugh was a narcissist—he wasn't about to kill himself. So, he had decided that the solution to his problem was to get rid of Elizabeth. He felt that divorce was out of the question because in his mind, he was too proud and upstanding to go through an ugly divorce in court. That would be fodder for the Kinder County gossipers to use to devour him, and his good name would be tarnished in the eyes of the people who admired and respected him. After all, most people in Anderson nearly worshipped the ground Elizabeth walked on.

High, knowing he had sizeable insurance coverage on Elizabeth, had finally decided that an accidental death would be the best route to take because the double indemnity clause would add another million dollars to his coffers. He could use that money to spoil Agatha the way the young, sweet, beautiful nymph should be spoiled. He felt that if he would shower her with all the worldly goods she desired, she would overlook the fact that he was so much older and lacking the machismo of his youth. After all, it was a known fact that Agatha slept around with men of pseudo-stature who had the means to pay her for services rendered.

Hugh began plotting Elizabeth's demise. He decided that the best cover-up for his dirty deed would be a fire. And since this was January and a time when everyone was warming their homes with hot fires, an accident of a fiery nature would provide the perfect obscurant for his misdeed. Although he had a two or three month window to carry out his plan, Hugh was anxious to get it over and done with because he ached to have Agatha all to himself now. He felt he couldn't wait another day because he could not stomach the idea of Agatha being touched by other men. Even though Hugh knew that Agatha was a whore, his desire for her was so strong that it really did not matter to him what she was. He was going to make a major change in his lifestyle by marrying her—at least that's what he thought. It did not matter to him that he would become the laughingstock of Kinder County. Nothing mattered to him now except his lust for Agatha.

Agatha was only 21 years old, while Hugh was 58. At his age, Hugh's virility was declining while Agatha's muliebrity had not even peaked. How on earth he ever thought he could keep her satisfied is one of the great mysteries of life. But he did. So he pressed on.

Elizabeth had just passed her 50th birthday and her youthful beauty, in Hugh's eyes, had long faded. The traces of gray in her hair were growing more noticeable with each passing day. She was developing soft lines in her skin and the crow's feet around her beautiful blue eyes had deepened. To any onlooker, Elizabeth was still a beautiful woman. If Hugh chose to divorce her, no doubt Elizabeth would have a wealth of suitors. She was still vital and energetic, and carried with her one of the most pleasant personalities a lady could wear. She was totally unsuspecting that the love of her life had set his sights on a younger beauty—albeit a woman of questionable character.

Agatha was totally unaware of Hugh's plans to get rid of Elizabeth. The only significance that Agatha attached to Hugh was simply that he was a good Sugar Daddy—someone who had the means to pay for what she was selling. And Hugh was a real good customer. Agatha often wondered how Hugh could entertain her at least three nights per week, knowing he had a loving wife at home. But Agatha didn't dwell on those thoughts whenever they crossed her mind because she hardly worried about the consequences of her own actions, so she definitely did not channel her thoughts into the affairs of other people. She was young, carefree, and an opportunist. Whenever and wherever there was an opportunity to earn a buck, Agatha took it, with pleasure.

Unlike Elizabeth, who had grown up surrounded by, and showered with wealth, Agatha was from a poor family of sharecroppers. As Agatha watched her parents struggle to provide for herself and her siblings, she vowed she would never be a poor struggling woman like her mother. She knew her mother was a good Christian woman, and her daddy was a good, loving, hard-working man, but their goodness and Christianity and hard work never got them out of a rut. So, Agatha sought another route to better herself.

Agatha had heard tales all during her childhood about Miss Circe and the girls who lived with her in Hawk Town. She knew what they did to earn their keep. While she planned to one day approach Miss Circe about employment, in the meantime she had found that she could single handedly earn her keep in her own little town by entertaining the men who would sneak around and cheat on their wives. In Agatha's young mind, how those men handled themselves at home with their wives was none of her business. As long as they met her in secrecy and paid for services rendered, all was well.

As Agatha pondered her idea of one day asking Miss Circe for employment, she didn't know if she would be accepted. After all, the ladies, if you could call them ladies, who worked for Miss Circe were African-American or Native American and Agatha had no idea whether or not a white girl would be welcomed to join their bordello. In the meantime, the back seat of cars, bed of pickup trucks, barn floors, hay lofts, or grass were fine for the business at hand. One reason she performed for old Hugh was he had a comfortable guest house in the back of his mansion where she would meet him for their trysts. So she knew that at least three nights of her week would be spent in splendor compared to the other unsuitable sacks where she immersed herself as a lady of the night.

If Agatha had known what Hugh was planning for her, she would have laughed in his face. What would make a man of 58 think that a hot number like her who was only 21 want to spend the rest of her life with him? Who knows how many years she might have to tolerate and care for an old man of his stature? It could only be described as foolishness, and it is difficult for rational-thinking people to understand the ways and actions of fools. What inclines them to conjure up their foolish tendencies and think deep in the box?

Hugh had to be certain that his plan for Elizabeth was foolproof. Hugh's opinion of Sheriff Zack Green was never high. He had the Kinder County Sheriff pegged as an arrogant birdbrain. He felt that Zack Green could easily be duped. However, the sheriff had staffed his department with some pretty sharp and smart younger deputies. So, Hugh had to outfox a whole department and the coroner as well if he was going to do his dirty deed and get away scot-free.

Now, the coroner who served Kinder County was no dimwit. He was sought after by numerous jurisdictions for his investigative acumen and problem-solving techniques. He was a Harvard graduate, and for the life of Hugh, he could not understand why John Riverbank returned to the South to practice his skills in Kinder and surrounding counties. But John Riverbank was a native of Kinder County who had always loved living in the country, as opposed to running the rat race in the city. Upon graduating from high school, he had been accepted by a number of Ivy League universities, and he only left the South to get the best possible education. Once he had earned his degrees, he could hardly wait to return home. He had been fed up with elitist attitudes and persnickety behaviors, and had been anxious to return to an area where people were down-to-earth.

While still in Cambridge, John had seen the job posting for a coroner's position in Old Thumover County. He immediately applied and was selected from a pool of highly qualified applicants. He was overjoyed when he received the appointment letter only two weeks after he had been interviewed for the position, and left Cambridge immediately to begin a new venture. He left so suddenly that he did not take the time to pack his scarce belongings. He left everything and told his friends to take what they wanted and give the rest to the Salvation Army.

John not only loved his job as coroner, he loved living in Old Thumover County. It was contiguous to Kinder County and John relished being close to his homestead and family. He was only a 25-mile drive from his parents' home.

Hugh knew John Riverbank's family well. The Mansons and the Riverbanks had been family friends for nearly five generations. While Hugh deplored the situation he was destined to create for John—the entanglement of analyzing the cause of a house fire and subsequent death of Elizabeth--his plan was the best option, in Hugh's mind, to resolving the problem of how to rid himself of a wife who now stood in his way of eternal bliss. Nothing was going to stop him from executing his horrendous plan.

Hugh chose Wednesday night to carry out his doomsday plan because on Wednesday nights most men of his community got inebriated at the local clubs, joints or hangouts, while the ladies of the community were engaged in Bible Study. This meant there would hardly be any one around to notice the fire until it was well out of control. Hugh's estate was expansive, and the Manson home set back 300 yards from the main road, and was surrounded by cedar, spruce, and magnolia trees. From the main road, the home was hardly visible through the vegetation.

All day on Wednesday, January 20th, Hugh was restless. Even though he had all materials in place for effectively ensuring a fast burn once he started the fire, Hugh was still nervous. At home he paced so much that Elizabeth asked him several times whether or not anything was wrong. Hugh assured his wife that all was well, that he was mentally planning crop rotation as it was approaching the time for clearing fields in preparation for planting what would become spring crops. Elizabeth offered Hugh a cup of tea to settle his nerves, which he readily accepted.

Later in the afternoon, Hugh drove downtown. Anderson was quiet because the cold weather tended to keep people inside warming by pot-belly heaters and fireplaces. Hugh suddenly remembered he needed more kerosene because even though he had stockpiled the fuel to be used that night, his neighbor had borrowed some of the fuel with a promise that he would replace it at the end of the month. That was in 11 more days, and Hugh intended to pull off his deed this very night.

Hugh drove his new 1954 black Hudson the few miles to the general store, entered the general store, and casually chatted with the few customers who were milling around inside. After assuring himself that he had engaged everyone in polite chitchat, he made his purchase—kerosene, more matches, and a roll of cheesecloth.

When he returned home, Hugh left the incendiary material in his vehicle. He decided he would try taking a nap so he would not have to think about what he was planning to do come nightfall, nor would he have to listen to Elizabeth's meaningless chatter for the remainder of the afternoon. Elizabeth, in the meantime, busied herself with completing the quilt that she had begun piecing together during the last ladies' group quilting session. Elizabeth's tenterhooks were on the top shelf in the hall closet, so she had to bother Hugh to get them for her. She was uneasy about getting on a stepladder.

Over at the general store, Oscar Watkins made a comment about Hugh's behavior when Hugh had come into the store a few hours earlier. Oscar, it seems, thought that Hugh was over-extending himself to be kind to everyone there. Oscar had never known Hugh to bother giving what he considered his underlings the time of day, and certainly not any semblance of common chitchat. Oscar seemed a bit puzzled by Hugh's simple act of kindness, although no one else at the general store had given a second thought to Hugh's communication with them.

***

When nightfall came and everyone was engaged in their usual Wednesday night activities, Hugh set his plan in motion. He was sure that after Elizabeth was in bed and asleep she was not going to wake up easily because he had politely offered her a cup of tea after dinner. It was a different flavor of tea than Elizabeth had made for him earlier in the day. Hugh laced Elizabeth's tea with St. John's wort because Hugh knew that the taste was comparable to black tea and blended well with a variety of flavors. Once Hugh checked on Elizabeth and knew she was asleep, he began to soak the downstairs floors with kerosene and then covered all the floors with cheesecloth. Since the bedrooms were upstairs, Hugh knew there was no way Elizabeth could escape the burning house because even if she woke up and tried to get out, the upstairs windows had been sealed shut, as usual, for the winter months.

When Hugh was satisfied that all the wood downstairs was saturated with the flammable liquid, he went out to the guest house and changed all of his clothes, including his shoes. After he had dressed, he put the clothes he had been wearing in a laundry sack, got his box of matches, and went back to the house. He opened the door to the mudroom, lit the bag of clothes he was holding, and threw it into the kitchen. He left the mudroom door open as he headed back to the guest house. From his perch on the front porch of the guest house, he could see the flames spreading throughout the first level of his home. He silently prayed that the smoke would kill Elizabeth before she could wake up, and that Elizabeth would die a painless death. He did not want her to feel the pain of being burned. Hugh knew that it would be a while before anyone saw smoke coming from their home, so he waited until the house was totally engulfed in flames before he began ringing the fire alarm bell that stood near the top of his old well that was no longer being used to draw water from below the ground surface.

Agatha was actually the first person to hear the bell, because this being Wednesday night, she was already on her way to the Manson's guest house for their usual Wednesday night tryst. Agatha began running and screaming. Her screams could be heard by everyone within earshot of the Manson home. Neighbors heard the screams and the bell that was the signal that somewhere a fire was burning out of control. As they ran outside, a blaze at the Manson home could be seen through the trees and underbrush. By this time, everyone who could see the blaze realized that there was nothing that could be done to save the house. It was totally engulfed, and the roof was beginning to cave in.

People of the community began to wonder if Hugh and Elizabeth had gotten out of the house safely. The question was partially answered when Hugh came running from the guest house. He appeared visibly shaken as he screamed that Elizabeth was in the house. "Oh, my God! Please help me!" he cried. Within eight minutes after the alarm sounded, Sheriff Zack Green's cruiser had arrived on the scene and he brought the vehicle to a screeching halt. He jumped out and ran to Hugh. Hysterically, Hugh was telling him that Elizabeth did not get out. Hugh stated that he had fallen asleep in the guest house as that was his custom on Wednesday nights while Elizabeth attended Bible Study. He explained that she had not attended Bible Study this night because she was feeling poorly. Hugh stated that Elizabeth had drunk a cup of tea early in the night and gone to bed. That's when, according to Hugh, he left the mansion and went to the guest house.

Nearly everyone in the community knew that Hugh hung out in the guest house on Wednesday nights. And almost everyone knew why, except Elizabeth. So Hugh thought to himself that he was in the clear. Neighbors were offering to help Hugh in any way they could. They were expressing condolences because he had lost Elizabeth. It was a sad and painful fact for everyone who knew her. Even Agatha was grieving the loss of Elizabeth. But she was uncharacteristically grieving more for Hugh. Agatha had no idea that Hugh was the responsible culprit for all the destruction surrounding them. She did not know that Hugh had devised this plan in order to have her permanently in his life.

As the crowd continued to swell outside of Hugh's burning home, Hugh's roving eyes were searching for Agatha. He spotted her in the arms of Oscar Watkins, who seemed to have been consoling her because she appeared to be genuinely upset. At the sight of Agatha wrapped in Oscar's arms, Hugh became incensed with jealousy. He was so angry he could hardly contain himself from walking over to them and snatching Agatha away from Oscar. Hugh felt it was he who should be holding Agatha, but he could not act on his passion because he was supposed to be grieving over the fact that he had just lost his wife. Oscar, however, did not miss the dirty look Hugh was giving him, and he purposely made eye contact with Hugh. He wanted Hugh to see the smirk on his face as a telltale sign to Hugh that he knew Hugh was insanely jealous of his cradling Agatha his arms.

Hours later, when the fire had been extinguished and the fire coals were smoldering, Sidney, a neighbor, invited Hugh to come home with him and sleep in his guest room until things were somewhat settled. Hugh thanked him for the offer, but assured Sidney that he would be OK living out back in his own guest house until other arrangements could be made. Hugh was thinking he needed Agatha in the sack more now than ever before because his desire for her was incessant, and there was nothing standing in the way of his fulfillment now that Elizabeth was gone.

***

When John Riverbank received the call that he was needed in Anderson at the Manson residence where a fire had taken the life of Elizabeth Manson, he was visibly shaken. He had known Elizabeth for such a long time and it was hard for him to fathom that she was no longer alive. John broke the speed limit as he headed to Anderson, making the 25-minute drive in only 15 minutes. When he arrived on the scene, Sheriff Green and few other law enforcement officers had taped off the area with police tape to prevent anyone from disturbing the scene before fire investigators could determine what had caused the fire, and before the coroner could examine what remained of Elizabeth's body.

One of the officers approached John immediately and stated that the smell of kerosene was profuse around the perimeter of the burned-out house. He had also noticed several kerosene kegs in back of the shed in the rear of the property appeared to have been recently moved. He noticed fresh footprints in that area. Given that tidbit of information, John's antenna went up because he and his family had visited the Manson residence a month earlier when they had been invited to dinner after church one Sunday. The Mansons used wood in the fireplaces, and used strips of lightwood kindling as fire starters. There would not have been any reason to use kerosene in the home. John was instantly suspicious because during the course of his studies at Harvard, a great deal of time had been devoted to studying corpses where the cause of death appeared to be a house fire, but upon thorough examination, had been killed by other means and the fire had been set as a cover up. John hoped that this was not the case in Elizabeth's death. He would use everything at his disposal to see that an exhaustive and accurate autopsy was performed.

***

The throng had begun to scatter at the remains of the Manson home because by this time it was after midnight—long past the bedtime of most country folks. Hugh, however, was anything but sleepy. Actually, he was horny because Wednesday night was his night to romp in the sheets with Agatha. He looked around and spotted her leaving with Oscar. Hugh could not contain himself. He yelled out her name and a hush came over the crowd as heads turned from Hugh to Agatha. Agatha stopped abruptly in her tracks, pulled away from Oscar, and just stood immobilized. She was shocked that Hugh would blatantly call out her name at a time when he should be decimated by his loss. Agatha knew that everyone was looking and listening to see how she would respond. She was certain that her Wednesday night trysts with Hugh were no secret to most of the citizens of Anderson. She whispered to Oscar to go on without her. She was not going to risk losing her best-paying customer, and she had no idea what Hugh had done.

The coroner was paying very close attention to this drama as it played out. Hugh's crying out to Agatha elevated John's suspicion to a much higher level. So, without being obvious, he watched closely to see how Hugh and Agatha interacted after Hugh had called her name. He noticed Agatha whispering something to Oscar and then, after standing numbly for a few moments, she walked in the direction of the Mansons' guest house.

To be certain that the murder of his wife would be accepted as an accident, Hugh protested vehemently when John Riverbank pointed out that the actual cause of Elizabeth's death could not be determined with any accuracy until the pathologist had completed an autopsy. The coroner told Hugh it would be futile to make funeral arrangements over the next several days because, being the only available pathologist, he had a backlog of autopsies John was analyzing and he would not be free to take a look at Elizabeth's case until the following Monday, and today was Thursday. Hugh was livid. He ranted overblown inconsequential, downright lame excuses as to why he had to bury his wife's remains immediately. John Riverbank was not wavering in his decision. He suggested to Hugh that he calm down and perhaps visit his family physician for a prescription of tranquilizers to steady his nerves. Hugh, at that moment, was a shattered individual.

***

In the past, knowing that Elizabeth was alive, and there was a possibility that she might return home early one Wednesday night and decide to visit Hugh at the guest house, added an air of excitement which had always thrilled Agatha mischievously. In fact, that was one of the sentiments that made sleeping with Hugh more tingling. It certainly was not his machismo as Hugh narcissistically believed. As Agatha had wormed her way into the guest house and lay in wait for Hugh to complete his business with the coroner and Sheriff

Green, she had decided that this night would mark the end of her stealthy meetings with Hugh.

After what seemed like an eternity, Hugh, wearing an expression of despair, slunk into their love nest. He was exhausted, yet still randy for Agatha. When he reached for her, she raised up on her elbows and told Hugh that they needed to talk. Hugh sat on the side of the bed and began rubbing her thighs and kissing, actually squeezing her flesh with an intensity, which usually excited Agatha, but now repulsed, rather than excited, his paramour. While Hugh continued his lustful action, Agatha again said, "Hugh, we need to talk!" Although he wasn't in the mood for anything except making love to Agatha, Hugh's eyes met hers and he paused. There was a peevish look on Agatha's face that seemed untrustworthy and foreboding. It mirrored a premonition of trouble. Hugh didn't need any trouble from Agatha at the moment because, unbeknownst to him, John Riverbank's suspicion, in conjunction with Sheriff Green's collaboration with fire investigators and the fire marshal relative to Elizabeth's death, a firestorm of a different kind was on the brink of raging for Hugh. An autopsy would be necessary.

"What is it? What's the matter?" Hugh inquired.

"We need to cool it for a while."

"Why?"

"Because it just makes sense for me to stay away from you until all of your affairs pertaining to the fire are in order. After all, you are a grieving widower now."

Hugh seized Agatha by her shoulders and asked, "What's that got to do with us?" He noticed what appeared to be a smirk, or maybe a look of consternation, of Agatha's face. He pulled her close and whispered menacingly, "I did this for us!" Agatha was speechless and suddenly frightened. The implication of that statement was terrifying to her. She began shaking all over and began to hyperventilate. Now, she understood why the investigating officers were so concerned about the scent of kerosene in the air. All of a sudden the thought occurred to her that Hugh had killed his wife and used the fire to cover up his malefaction. "Oh, no!" she thought. And what if he had burned Elizabeth alive? Agatha knew that she could never trust this man again. If he could so callously rid himself of his wife who loved, admired, and practically worshipped him, he could do the same to her without giving it a second thought. In an instant, Hugh became Agatha's worst nightmare, and she knew she needed to get away from him immediately. From now on, Hugh would no longer be a customer of hers, and she would avoid him at all costs.

Hugh was a man that Agatha really cared nothing for except his money. She told Hugh his grip was hurting her and he loosened it slightly. Agatha tremulously said she needed to leave because her mother would be wondering where she was and would be worried about her. Because even though her mother was aware of the manner in which she spent her time, which gave cause for worrying, Agatha never stayed out all night. She had made a promise to her mother that she would always be home before sunrise, once her mother had understood that Agatha was going to flirt with men as a means of supporting herself. Agatha always tried to convince her mother that her profession was not dangerous. But her mother knew better.

The punctilious Hugh voiced a deep-seated need to make love to Agatha. "I need you right now more than ever," he said.

"No, Hugh! I need to leave this minute!" Agatha cried. Hugh responded by slapping Agatha so hard that she felt as if she had been struck in the face by a club. The shock Agatha felt was jolting. She was appalled that Hugh would lose his temper with her in what should have been his hour of humbleness and disconsolation.

She had never seen anything but the gentle side of his character. Agatha became uneasy and wanted to escape the situation as it was unfolding. She was gradually realizing that Hugh had a darker persona that he had kept hidden behind a façade of civility throughout the time she had cavorted with him. In essence, Hugh was a hypocrite in love. Agatha had always known he was arrogant, but until tonight, she had never seen his surly side. During the entire time Agatha had been using Hugh, she had him pegged as a pushover, an all-day sucker.

As fear began to slowly creep through Agatha's veins, she began to feel a revulsion toward Hugh, and a strong sense of urgency to get away from him. She knew she needed to escape this old man's grip by any means necessary. She pretended to give in to his desire and began rubbing Hugh, whispering sultry, arousing declarations to him, and telling him how sorry she was for the situation he was in—with losing his home and his wife. She suggested that they do a quickie so she could get home to her mom before sunrise. She faked passion while Hugh had his way with her.

When Agatha left the Manson guest house she was thinking about Hugh's demeanor, in particular she was trying to decipher the meaning of the statement he had made: "I did this for us!" The implication of the statement was terrifying to her. She began to run. At the same time, her entire body was shaking and trembling. Now she understood why the investigating officers were so concerned about the scent of kerosene around the burned-out house. It hit her like a ton of bricks that Hugh had killed his wife and used the fire to cover up his malefaction! Agatha knew she could never trust Hugh again not to harm her. Because if he could rid himself of the wife in such a brutal fashion--who loved, admired, and practically worshipped him—he would not think twice about harming or getting rid of her. As a matter of fact, the anger that she had seen in him only a few minutes earlier was proof that Hugh would rid himself of her to ensure his own weal. Hugh had suddenly become her worst nightmare! She knew from this day forward she needed to avoid Hugh at all costs.

When Agatha reached her home at 3:30 that Thursday morning, her mother was wide awake. She had heard the sirens of police cruisers, an ambulance and, of course, numerous fire engines. Fire departments from Highlow, Sassafras Corner, and East Kinder had responded to the call for assistance from the Anderson Fire and Rescue Squad. She was relieved to see Agatha walking through the door, because with all the pandemonium in the vicinity, she naturally was concerned whether or not Agatha was involved in a catastrophe since she had not arrived home yet.

After Agatha had settled down and calmed herself with a shot of blueberry brandy, she shared the details of the tragedy with her mother. Agatha told her mother she suspected Hugh Manson was in deep trouble and she did not want to be associated with him anymore. Because, she said, she had seen a side of Hugh tonight that really frightened her, and she was anxious to get away from him. Agatha explained that for a long time she had been contemplating seeking employment at Miss Circe's Place located in the Hawk Town Community of Granite Point. And although it was nearly 30 miles from Anderson, if she were lucky enough that Miss Circe would take her in, she would be able to visit with Gertrude, at least every two weeks. She was sure some John would gladly give her a ride in exchange for a favor.

Miss Gertrude, Agatha's mother, reluctantly agreed with Agatha's plan. That being settled, Agatha was anxious to approach Miss Circe as soon as possible, and she wanted to be driven to Hawk Town that very day. But Miss Gertrude told her that she looked too haggard, with dark circles under her eyes from lack of sleep, and her hair smelled smoky, and she just did not appear presentable enough to ask to be considered for a job of that nature. Miss Gertrude suggested that Agatha get cleaned up—"bathe and wash your hair," she said. "And then lie down and get some much needed rest. Today is Thursday; we can drive there tomorrow around noon and perhaps Miss Circe will accept you since it's the weekend, and her business really booms Friday, Saturday, and Sunday nights."

Miss Gertrude was making perfect sense to Agatha. But that was no surprise because her mother, even though poor, and for all intents and purposes, a sharecropper, had always been a wise woman.

The very next day, at 11 o'clock, Miss Gertrude and Agatha got into Miss Gertrude's old 1941 Packard Clipper and headed east to Granite Point. They arrived at Miss Circe's Place just as the clock struck 12 o'clock mid-day. The timing was perfect because some of the girls were relaxing on the front porch, so Agatha got a cursory look at how they dressed and a quick glance at how they were made up. Agatha could match their sleazy bedizened attire because Hugh had brought her lots of pieces for a sleazy wardrobe because he loved to see her dress as a floozy. It really turned him on to see her dressed that way, and then have her undress for him.

Agatha told the girls that she was there because she would like to speak with Miss Circe. They looked at Agatha as if they were assessing her worthiness to join them. After a few awkward moments, one of the harlots asked Agatha to follow her. Miss Gertrude had remained seated in the car. The girl who led Agatha to Miss Circe's office was named Lola. She knocked on the door to Miss Circe's office and said there was someone there to see her if she had a few minutes.

Miss Circe invited them to come in. Miss Circe was pleasantly surprised to see a white girl in her office, and she was hoping that the girl was seeking employment, because some of her newer customers had been specifically asking for what they referred to as "white meat." Lola excused herself as Miss Circe invited Agatha to take a seat.

"Now tell me, what's on your mind, young lady?" Miss Circe inquired. Agatha clearly stated that she was seeking employment. She shared her background with Miss Circe, giving her details about Hugh Manson and how he had kept her for several years, but now she needed to get away from Hugh, but had no other means of gaining a steady income for herself. She humbled herself to Miss Circe and promised that she would do a good job for her if Miss Circe would give her a chance to prove herself.

As Miss Circe sized her up, it was plain to see that Agatha was a beautiful girl. She had very pale skin and fiery red hair. She was tall; Miss Circe guessed her to be 5 foot, 9 or 10 inches, slender, green-eyed, and somewhat charming. She would be a welcomed addition to her house of ill repute. With all the extra new business that would be coming to her from the new men in town working construction, Agatha could not have arrived at a better time.

Miss Circe outlined her expectations of the girls and told Agatha about the layout of the house. She handed Agatha a list of expectations and discussed each item on the list with her, instructing Agatha to ask questions about anything she did not understand. Agatha appeared to glean the operation as delineated. When Miss Circe had covered everything on the list, she asked Agatha, again, if she had any questions, and Agatha did not.

"When could you start?" Miss Circe inquired. "That is, if I decide to give you a try." Agatha stated she could begin immediately once she went back home and gathered a few of her things. Miss Circe was pleased and wanted to know how Agatha had gotten there. Agatha explained that her mother had brought her and was waiting outside in her car.

Miss Circe stood, came around her desk, and put her hand on Agatha's shoulder. She escorted Agatha out to her mother's vehicle and introduced herself. Miss Circe assured Miss Gertrude that she would take good care of Agatha. She told her not to worry because she protected all of her girls. Miss Circe told Miss Gertrude that she would be sending a driver to get Agatha at 6 o'clock that evening. It was now 2:30 in the afternoon.

Both Agatha and her mother were suffused with happiness as they drove away from the big house. All the fear and apprehension that Agatha had felt on the drive to Miss Circe's had practically vanished. Agatha and Miss Gertrude were relaxed on the return trip home.

As soon as Miss Gertrude had parked the Packard and she and Agatha were inside the house, Agatha went to her closet and began pulling out the sleazy, sexy, slinky clothes that befitted the image of a harlot. Over a two-year period she had gotten plenty experience wearing and modeling them for Hugh. Agatha was looking forward to a change of venue, as well as broadening her conquests. Who knew? One day she might even find a man she cared about who would love her in return and retire her from the only profession she knew.

As Agatha continued packing, Gertrude was thinking that Hugh wouldn't dare have the nerve to come looking for Agatha, but if he did, she would deny knowing where Agatha had gone. As far as Gertrude was concerned, Agatha's whereabouts would be her secret.

***

After several hours, the sheriff's investigators decided they had collected all of the evidence that could be gathered using artificial lighting in the darkened night. They would leave now and return later during daylight hours. They had observed Hugh returning to his guest cottage and knew that Agatha was in there with him. They would ask Hugh to come to Marigold to be interviewed at the sheriff's department, and if he refused, they could interrogate him on the spot at the cottage; and if it could be determined that they had enough evidence to link him to the suspected arson and charge him with Elizabeth's suspected murder, they would take Hugh into custody, lock him up, and ask the Judge to render a no-bail ruling.

Hugh, in his arrogance, had decided that he was in the clear. His assumption was that the fire had erased any evidence that might cause the investigating detectives to point the finger at him, or consider him a suspect in the alleged crime. Shucks! They didn't even know that a crime had been committed.

Hugh was unaware of the fact that John Riverbank and some of the sheriff's deputies, including the detectives, had him on the radar as a suspect. The sleuths gave deferential attention to John Riverbank's judgment in these types of situations because they were aware of, and respected, the fact that he had received his formal education and training from one of the nation's leading Ivy League universities. So, they were amenable and open-minded to John's initial on-site appraisal whenever there was suspicion in a case that a crime had been committed. With the kerosene that had been used as an accelerant, who else could have committed such a heinous act on the Manson property? Who would benefit from Elizabeth's death except Hugh? As far as John Riverbank was concerned, this case was no whodunit because it was obvious that Hugh was the perpetrator of this unspeakable crime.

John would examine Elizabeth's remains—what bit there was left of her—and if his findings indicated that she had been murdered as he suspected, he would implore Zack to arrest Hugh and see that he was prosecuted to the fullest extent that the law allowed and never see daylight again. John didn't care how rich Hugh was; he was not above the law and John felt Hugh's punishment should be severe to match the severity of the crime Hugh had committed.

Later the same morning, the town's folk in Marigold had heard about the fire at the Hugh Manson estate. The worst gossipers in town were abuzz in habitual fashion, spreading hearsay and innuendos about what did, might have, or was going to happen in the dreadful situation.

Around 2 o'clock, the two investigating detectives who had left the scene of the fire in Anderson and had gone home to get a few hours of sleep, returned to the sheriff's department and were at their respective desks plowing through the evidence they had collected, and were reviewing some of the statements they had captured from listening to, and in some cases eavesdropping on, people who had come, for various reasons, to the fire at the Manson home. Some had come in earnest to help put the fire out, or at least contain it to the house and keep it from spreading to other property. Some folks had come simply to be among the throng as this was perhaps the most excitement they had seen in months. Some folk were known as ambulance chasers and whenever they heard a siren, they had a need to know not only what had happened, and who it had happened to. Sometimes, they were sympathetic to the victim or victims, and sometimes not. In the case of Hugh Manson, there were some of both.

Those who were jealous of the Mansons' wealth had no sympathy for the worldly goods and material Hugh had lost. However, they were sorry that Sweet Miss Elizabeth had lost her life. People who were employed by Hugh and worked on his farm were concerned about their jobs in terms of whether or not Hugh's faculties would still be sound and he would be capable of giving them proper guidance and instructions on his plans for planting this year—because in six weeks it would be time to begin burning fields and making the grounds ready to open up to the seeds that needed to be planted. And then there were some people who were totally indifferent to Hugh and his wealth, and couldn't care less one way or the other.

After several hours at the office, the investigating detectives decided it was time to go speak with Hugh. They had given him enough time, in their opinion, to get some sleep, and now it was time to get down to some serious business.

When the detectives drove up to the front of the Manson guest house, Hugh was sitting on the front steps staring into space. He presented a disheveled appearance—he hadn't shaved, or combed his hair, and was wearing old slippers and no socks. The outside temperature was only 40 degrees Fahrenheit, which begged anyone to wear proper clothing. Hugh was wearing a thin cotton shirt, but was not covered in a sweater or jacket.

As the detectives exited their department-issued, plain gray four-door Ford, Hugh looked in their direction but did not speak. So, the detectives spoke to Hugh and asked if he was willing to speak with them for a few minutes. Hugh stood up, nodded in the affirmative, and invited them inside where the cottage was warm and cozy.

When one of the detectives told Hugh that they were there to try and get more details about what caused the fire and Elizabeth's death, Hugh said all he knew was that it was an accident. He said he didn't know what caused the accident because he had fallen asleep here in the cottage. He said he awakened and saw that the house was on fire. He said he ran to the cast iron bell that is used for sounding an alarm and began ringing it to bring help. He said at that point the entire house was ablaze and there was no way for him to get inside to see if Elizabeth was trapped inside. Hugh continued on by saying he yelled Elizabeth's name repeatedly, and he kept hoping to see her running around the side of the house to let him know that she was OK. But that did not happen. Hugh stated that he didn't remember very much after that.

The investigators listened carefully to every word coming from Hugh's mouth. One of the investigators was continuously taking notes as Hugh was speaking. Once they returned to the sheriff's department, they would wait for the fire marshal's report, because they kept in the forefront of their minds the kerosene that had been so acrid and pungent in the air at the scene of the fire. That report, in conjunction with the coroner's report, should provide the evidence they needed to arrest Hugh and charge him with murder because Hugh's story was extremely shallow, considering the degree of devastation that had demolished his mansion so quickly. A house fire, under normal conditions—without the use of accelerants—would not have burned out as swiftly as it did at the Mansons' mansion. There was no further action for the detectives to take now, except wait.

John Riverbank's report indicated that Elizabeth had died from smoke inhalation. There wasn't very much the detectives could do with these results in terms of charging Hugh with murder. But this finding was not a last resort. They now needed to examine this case from the angle that Hugh committed the crime of arson that subsequently led to Elizabeth's death, meaning Hugh was purposely responsible for her demise. For what other reason would he have saturated the house with fuel and set it ablaze? Knowing that his wife was inside and would be trapped upstairs constituted cruel and unusual punishment.

To collect the evidence necessary for the arson charge, the investigators started out at the general store to check Hugh's purchases of fuel in recent weeks. In the process, they discovered that as recently as the night of the fire, Hugh had purchased fuel that very afternoon. Additionally, the store clerk said that Hugh had purchased more than 200 gallons of fuel four weeks prior. He said at the time, Hugh said that he was preparing to burn his fields to be ready for spring planting. The clerk said that amount of fuel was more than enough to cover the ground Hugh would be planting. The detectives asked for a copy of the receipts that the clerk duplicated and signed. The clerk stated that if the original receipts were needed, they could make a switch.

When all the necessary evidence had been gathered, the detectives were issued a warrant for Hugh Manson's arrest. The charges included arson and murder. The arrest of Hugh Manson was going to be the most astounding news in recent years in Kinder County. Most folks would not believe it.

Zack Green and the two detectives arrested Hugh at 1:30 in the afternoon. Surprisingly, Hugh did not ask any questions and did not offer any resistance. Hugh spent his first of what would become many nights in jail because no bond had been set. Hugh slept through the night, and the next morning ate the breakfast he was served. By 10 o'clock, his attorney, Drifton Moss, had received word of Hugh's arrest, and he went to the jail to visit Hugh. What Drift saw was a fallen man. Hugh wasn't even a shadow of the man he once was. He appeared to have hit rock bottom.

Drift told Hugh he would do all that was possible to help him, but Hugh had to share with him anything that would aid in his defense. Hugh had nothing to offer. Hugh said, "Let's get this over as soon as possible."

Drift told Hugh that it appeared he would be behind bars until his trial because no bond had been set for his release. Hugh said, "Fine!" And he fell silent again.

Drift said he would bring papers for Hugh to sign giving permission to cremate Elizabeth's remains, and that they would be placed in a plot at the cemetery. Again, Hugh made no response.

A few days later, Elizabeth's ashes were buried in a marble container. There was no one present except her minister who offered a prayer for her soul. The very same day, Drift Moss returned to the jail to inform Hugh that Elizabeth was in a final resting place. Hugh made no response. So, Drift got up to leave, and Hugh finally said, "I need to tell you something."

Drift returned to his seat and gave Hugh his undivided attention. Hugh said, without remorse, "I killed Elizabeth. Will you do whatever is necessary to let me make my plea before the court and get on with my life?"

Drift Moss presented a temporary insanity plea on Hugh's behalf when the time came. Hugh was given a life sentence without provision for parole.

PART III

During the early years of the decade that began in 1950, there was a boom in new school construction because children born to "Baby Boomers" had reached the mandatory age to begin their education. This growth in the student population brought about a phasing out of schools functioning as one-room schools. New multi-classroom schools were being built all across America. At the same time, soldiers were returning home from the war anxious to re-enter life with paramours or get married and begin a new family lifestyle using the G.I. Bill that had been signed into law by President Franklin D. Roosevelt on June 22, 1944, which enabled the recently discharged soldiers to get a head start in life. The G.I. Bill provided funds for a college education, unemployment insurance, and housing for veterans of the Second World War.

Many of the returning soldiers accepted construction jobs because they were plentiful and there was a growing need to get new schools up and running to accommodate the influx of new 5- and 6-year-old children born to Baby Boomers. In combination, these factors stimulated an economical boost, the impact of which would be felt for years to come. And like the rest of the nation, Kinder County certainly capitalized from the new business ventures. Not only were new schools under construction, but new bridges were being built and new highways as well. Because so many new construction employees were coming to the area, a demand was created for bed and breakfast establishments, restaurants, and places where men could go to unwind.

Miss Circe was elevated in her informal role as the Queen of Hearts. Her business increased so much that she had to convert her three-car garage into three temporary bedrooms so that fewer pleasure-seekers would have to wait in line for fulfillment. It was a happy time for most citizens of Kinder County, and the nation as a whole, with few exceptions.

One of the new schools under construction was what would become Granite Point Elementary School. It was designed to accommodate students from grades 1 through 6. There was no kindergarten available at that time. It would be nearly two decades later before the State of Xenolina would institute kindergarten accommodations for early childhood development.

While everyone was excited about the new school that was beginning to take shape in Granite Point— parents, kids, and teachers alike—people had not forgotten about Clemis Stapleton's disappearance. It was the greatest mystery that had ever occurred in Kinder County. Almost everyone suspected that the murder of the two school teachers and Clemis' disappearance were somehow connected. This conclusion had been drawn because the coroner had consulted another forensic pathologist who had been able to determine, same as he had, that the cause of death was gunshot wounds as opposed to smoke inhalation and burns from the actual fire. All of the old men who frequented Buster's Place still believed that Clemis had made a fool of himself with the school teachers and had gone off the deep end and committed a crime that would surely have put him away for life. But rather than spend his remaining days on Earth incarcerated, Clemis had left town.

It was a shame how he had abandoned those 11 children and placed such a heavy burden on the older children weighting them down with the responsibility of rearing the younger kids. Thank God for a community of kind, loving neighbors who pitched in to help the Stapletons when it became apparent that Clemis was nowhere to be found and would probably not be returning to Hawk Town.

Teddy, Clemis' eldest son, had taken over the responsibilities of managing the farm, while the two oldest girls, Cora and Daisy, did a mighty fine job of taking care of the kids and household duties. It was as if the girls had a premonition that Clemis was never going to return to his home again. Teddy had never breathed a word about the note Clemis had left for him.

After he seemed to have gotten over the initial shock of his father's disappearance, Teddy had begun a steady courtship with Joyce Jones. The two of them appeared to be great for each other and their courtship could not have blossomed at a better time, because both of them had undergone a life-shattering experience and needed to be loved and to recapture a sense of security. Each of them brought fulfillment of those needs to the relationship for the other.

As time passed and Teddy and Joyce's relationship grew stronger, they began to discuss marriage. Teddy shared his plans with Joyce about purchasing the Martin house with money he had saved; and Joyce let him know that she had a nest egg that had been saved for her college education, which was now an impossible dream because she had to take care of her younger sisters. Together, they had decided that the best plan for them would be to get married quietly. Even though Joyce had always dreamed of having a big wedding one day when she got married, she was a sensible girl and knew that many times in life, some dreams must die. She wanted to marry Teddy and spend the rest of her life with him, and that was all that really mattered now after everything that had happened in their families.

In October, Joyce had her 18th birthday, and on that very day, she and Teddy drove to the town of Marigold, in which the Kinder County's center of government was located, and were married by the clerk of courts. Since they had not shared their plans with Joyce's sisters and Miss Circe and her circle of friends, nor had they told Teddy's family. So for a while, their marriage would be their secret.

A few months earlier, Joyce had gone to the Board of Education and completed an application to work at the new Granite Point Elementary School when it opened. It was projected to open to staff in June in order for preparations to be made for its grand opening for students at the beginning of the next school year, which would be somewhere between the first week to mid-August. Joyce had been promised a job as an administrative assistant.

Joyce would bubble with excitement when she thought about the fact that she had a new husband, and would soon have a new job that she believed she was going to broaden her sphere of happiness even more. She felt life was good in spite of the tragedies that had befallen both Teddy and her. She remembered a statement her daddy always made in times of trouble: "The Lord gives and the Lord takes away!" God had taken away her parents, but He had given her Teddy. And she was truly grateful for having him. She was going to be a good wife to him, and do everything within her power to keep him happy.

Joyce had decided that in the beginning, she and Teddy could furnish their home with the furniture that was owned by her parents. After all, their home had not been opened since the family tragedy that happened nearly one year ago. The home in which Joyce and her sisters had lived all their lives held some exquisite pieces of furniture that Briscoe had purchased over the years. Together, Joyce and Teddy had already decided that once they had closed the deal on the Martin house and moved in, Joyce's two sisters and Peggy, Teddy's youngest sister, would live with them. It would be a perfect arrangement. And living just across the field from the Stapleton home would serve to keep the two families solidified as one. Joyce, Cora, and Daisy had already discussed having outdoor dinners almost every evening beginning in late spring and continuing until early fall. Living somewhat communally this way would add zest to the humdrum days of country living, and would break the monotony that had plagued both families for the past seven or eight months. This way, the two families could effectuate a festive mood at the end of each day, lightening the atmosphere and overcoming any crestfallen experiences that might have percolated their day. The fact of the matter was that the long and close friendship that the Stapleton and Jones girls had enjoyed all of their lives would alleviate any notion that their plans did not follow the natural order of life's cycle.

After having made scrupulous plans for their future, Teddy and Joyce felt the time was ripe for letting Miss Circe and her circle of friends, and Teddy and Joyce's siblings, know that they were already husband and wife. They would invite Miss Circe to have dinner at the Stapleton home next Sunday evening and make the announcement with everyone present.

On Sunday, as planned, Cora, Daisy, and Joyce had prepared a scrumptious meal of fried chicken, baby back ribs, potato salad, a fresh garden salad, freshly baked rolls, crackers, iced tea and lemonade, with lemon meringue pie and chocolate cake for desserts. It was a country feast fit for the finest guest, and everyone earnestly considered Miss Circe, with all of her calculating and morally conflicting energy, as the finest. Joyce felt that she would never be able to repay Miss Circe for the kindness and compassion she had shown her and her sisters during their time of bereavement after having lost both their parents so tragically and unexpectedly. They would have been placed in a foster home with strangers had it not been for Miss Circe's generosity. They might have even been placed in separate foster homes, adding to the shock and pain they were experiencing at that time. Miss Circe had ingratiated herself into their hearts simply by the essence of her benevolence.

After everyone had been served, the kids took their food outdoors and ate picnic style while Teddy, Joyce, Cora, Daisy, and Miss Circe seated themselves in the formal dining room. When all appetites had been satiated, and before anyone left the table, Teddy said that Joyce and he had an announcement to make. He immediately took Joyce's hand in his and held everyone's individual attention. Then he announced that he and Joyce had been married since her 18th birthday two weeks ago. All the ladies were flabbergasted by the announcement, but they were exceedingly happy. While Joyce was sitting dreamily with a mile-wide smile spreading over her beautiful face, Miss Circe got up and hugged her, as Cora and Daisy were squeezing Teddy so tightly he could barely breathe. His sisters let him go and wrapped their arms around Joyce while Miss Circe hugged Teddy for the very first time ever. Outdoors, the kids, although playfully chattering and enjoying themselves, heard the commotion inside and ran to see what was happening in there. But they were met at the door because the five adults were coming outside to share the good news. It was a joyous Sunday evening.

When the excitement had slightly diminished, it was Miss Circe's turn to make an announcement. She told the clan that two months from this gathering, on Saturday, December 20th, Hawk Town friends and neighbors—the entire community—was going to witness the reception of the century. The guests of honor would be none other than Theodore and Joyce Jones Stapleton. When Joyce parted her lips to object, Miss Circe raised her hand and hushed Joyce before she could speak a word. Joyce was thinking that Miss Circe had already done so much for her, it would be an imposition to allow Miss Circe to do more. But Miss Circe had decided, and there was no changing her mind once she had made a decision.

Miss Circe told Cora, Daisy, and Joyce that they had only two months to plan the perfect reception. Decorating Miss Circe's place did not pose a problem because they would use a Christmas theme with holly, mistletoe, tinsels, the huge beautifully decorated tree that graced Miss Circe's foyer every year during the Christmas holidays, and they would serve a variety of hors d'oeuvres, cakes, and Christmas cookies; and wine, champagne, and punch for the kids. It was going to be the greatest reception to ever take place in the Hawk Town community.

Time seemed to have been moving at breakneck speed as plans for the reception got underway. While Miss Circe, Cora, and Daisy were concentrating on having all of the amenities in proper order, Joyce began looking for a dress that irresistibly appealed to her. She could choose any style of wedding dress because her young body was model svelte. She was 5 feet 10 inches tall and perfectly proportioned from head to toe. Joyce wanted a white dress that was without flair, yet designed to captivate attention and, most importantly, Teddy's attention. She felt that a white smooth satin dress with a touch of silvery lace would be perfect since it was so close to Christmas and the atmosphere would be sizzling with excitement and anticipation of the most celebrated day of the year. She felt a bouquet of lilies consisting of a mixture of calla, oxalis, and lily of the valley would capture both the spirit of love and the spirit of Christmas. More than anything, she wanted to look beautiful for Teddy and she wanted their reception to be as memorable as an elaborate wedding would have been. She planned to confer with Miss Circe to get approval of her idea, and she would ask Miss Circe if she could intersperse oxalis lilies among the poinsettias that would be placed throughout the great room, and the rest of the house.

By the time all plans had been finalized, and every detail in place, it was only two days remaining before the big event. All invitations had been mailed out no later than November 10th, and RSVPs had been received from 95 percent of the invitations that had been sent out. Joyce was both giddy and nervously anticipating her big day. While outwardly Teddy appeared to be calm, deep down he was nervous, too.

Everything was arranged as it should be for them. On November 3rd, they had gone to settlement on the Martin house. Afterward, they had begun a frantic cleanup for the next six days. After the interior of the house had been cleaned and painted with colors Joyce and the girls had selected, the men of the community had helped Teddy move furniture from the Jones house to Teddy and Joyce Stapleton's new home. When all was finished, the house was beautiful, comfortable, and begging to be lived in.

The girls, of course, had chosen pink for their bedroom. Joyce had chosen shades of blue for the master bath, and cream for the master bedroom. The guest room, which might one day become a nursery, was painted mint green. The girl's bathroom was all white, as was the kitchen. Joyce had chosen melon-colored café curtains for the kitchen that warmly welcomed anyone who entered. The living room and dining room walls were beige, and Joyce had chosen an array of colorful crushed velvet pillows to add some personal charm to the room; one for each arm chair, and three for the sofa. She had positioned her daddy's smooth brown leather recliner in the master bedroom near one of the windows for Teddy to claim at the end of each day. All things considered, Joyce was proud of the pastiche collection she had put together in their home. And Teddy had found a secondhand Adirondack porch swing in the thrift shop at the Granite Point crossroads, and had painted it white to match the white shutters he had added to all the windows. The shutters made an appealing contrast to the pewter gray color he had painted the exterior of their new home.

On the morning of December 20th, one would have thought it was Christmas Day already. At the Stapleton home, Teddy had laid out his dark suit and all of the clothes that his younger brothers would be wearing that day. The reception was scheduled to begin at 1 o'clock in the afternoon, and he knew that the boys should not get dressed up until 30 minutes before it was time for them to be driven to Miss Circe's house. He warned them not to horse around and get dirty after they had bathed that morning because there would be no time for a second bath when it was time to leave. The boys said they understood. After a late breakfast, they settled in front of the radio and listened to music and stories, colored pictures, and read until the noon day news came on. Then they knew it was time to get dressed.

Cora and Daisy had gotten everything ready for the girls. While they were all going to wear pretty new dresses for the occasion, Peggy would be the only one wearing a long, ruffled, red dress, since she was acting as a flower girl and junior hostess. She was proud of the title Miss Circe had given her, and she was over the moon about her new red formal gown. She even had red shoes to match, and she was the envy of her sisters, ages 11, 12, and 14.

Miss Circe had arranged for a local photographer to take a photograph of the entire Stapleton and Jones families once everyone arrived. He was pacing on the front steps when Miss Circe's chauffeur-driven Cadillac turned into the driveway. As the kids filed out, the photographer gave them instructions as to where he wanted each one to stand. He arranged them according to their height on the front steps of the mansion. It was going to be an award-winning wedding picture, even though the occasion was only a reception.

When all outdoor portraits had been taken, everyone was led to the great room. It was magnificent and had been professionally decorated. Its beauty literally took everyone's breath away, and they "ooohed and ahhhed" at this sight to behold.

Once all guests had arrived and people were mingling indoors as well as outside, it was plain to see that all who had come were having the time of their lives. Champagne, wine, and punch were plentiful. Shrieks of laughter and lots of chatter could be heard above the sounds of Brahms, Tchaikovsky, and Mendelssohn. As they wandered through the throng, making sure they had addressed everyone personally and thanked them for honoring them with their presence, Teddy and Joyce were inseparable.

After several hours, around 3 o'clock in the afternoon, Rev. Herman asked for everyone's attention and to join him in prayer as he prayed that Teddy and Joyce would live many happy years together and that God would bless them to be fruitful and multiply. Teddy and Joyce were overwhelmed by the outpouring of love and warmth their community had shown them.

At the end of what had been a heavenly day, and after the last guests had bid the happy couple farewell, Teddy and his brothers began loading gifts onto the bed of his old pickup truck, while all the girls piled into Miss Circe's big Cadillac. They were returning to their home, but Teddy would not be spending the night with them for the very first time. Tonight would serve as his wedding night and he and Joyce would be spending their first night together in their new home. They would have five full days of wedded bliss because the girls were not going to move in with them until the day after Christmas.

Teddy and his brothers unloaded the gifts at Teddy's new home, and then the boys would walk the short distance to their home. Before leaving they hugged Teddy, told him they loved him, and with laughter, wished him a happy honeymoon.

***

At the reception, in the midst of all the excitement, Dancie was having serious thoughts about opening the sandwich shop she had envisioned for many months. She felt the time was ripe since there were so many new opportunities in the area as a result of all the new construction and the potential clientele it was bringing to Kinder County. She had observed the ferocious appetites that the men working in the construction industry developed after a long hard day of work on the new school and the new highways and bridges. Her Uncle James had passed away last year, and since that time his soda shop had stood vacant. Perhaps her Aunt Nell would consider selling it to her. She felt certain that Aunt Nell could use the income because in the past, she had depended on income from the store, and now that income was no longer available to her. Even if Aunt Nell wouldn't sell the store, she might be willing to rent it to Dancie in order to generate a new source of monthly income for herself. Dancie planned to visit Aunt Nell first thing Monday morning.

As planned, by 9 o'clock Monday morning, Dancie was on her way to approach Aunt Nell with her plan. Dancie did not have to report to Buster's until 11 o'clock in order to prepare for the lunch crowd, so she had two full hours to convince Aunt Nell to either sell or rent the soda shop to her.

As it turned out, Aunt Nell loved the idea of Dancie's opening the building as a sandwich shop. Aunt Nell told Dancie she was not willing to sell the building at the present time, but she was definitely willing to rent it to her for a small monthly fee. Aunt Nell told Dancie her idea was an answer to her prayers, and she could take charge of the building immediately if she chose to do so.

Dancie explained that she would need to give Buster an adequate notice. Since this was the holiday season, business at Buster's Place was booming, and it would be that way until after Valentine's Day. So Dancie felt that for the next three months she owed it to Buster to be there for his business. She would give him a 90-day notice, and in the meantime, she would be getting the sandwich shop ready for a grand opening in the spring. She was bursting at the seams with excitement. She hugged Aunt Nell and promised to come visit her more frequently.

When Dancie arrived at Buster's Place, Buster was already there. She asked if he were available for her to speak to him briefly. Once they sat down, she told him what she was planning, and at first he seemed surprised.

Then he told her how much he appreciated her being considerate enough to remain in his employment throughout the holidays. He said anything he could do to help her get started, he was willing and would gladly do because she had been a godsend to him. He told her he felt that her new business would be a boost for his business because eating and drinking was what country folks loved to do. And they both smiled.

When the lunch crowd arrived, Buster shared Dancie's plans with the regulars, and each one of them promised Dancie that they would pitch in and help her get set up. She was happy to hear it because there was a tremendous amount of cleaning, painting, and yard work necessary before the sandwich shop's grand opening. They had three months to make all the essential preparations.

Spring is always aflutter with new hopes and dreams, and expectations of new life. One of the most exciting and pleasurable changes that brought new energy to Hawk Town in the spring was the grand opening and subsequent operation of Dancie's Sandwich Shop. From the day she opened, business exceeded all of her expectations. Word spread quickly about the new place in Hawk Town that sold food that was out-of-this-world delicious. Many of the sandwiches were foreign to country folks, and they loved the new delectable tastes. Everyone enjoyed both the ordinary and extraordinary flavors that delighted their palates. While Dancie's customers spanned the gamut from the very young to the elderly, her most dependable and constant customers were, surprisingly, teenagers. They loved the young refreshing atmosphere that Dancie had created; they loved the variety of foods she prepared and served; and they loved Dancie. Teens began to refer to Dancie's Sandwich Shop as Dancie's Place, and hearing them use the term so much, after six months of operation, Dancie replaced the sign that named her establishment Dancie's Sandwich Shop, with a new sign that simply called her place of business Dancie's Place.

One day as the teens were hanging outside around the six picnic tables Dancie had added to accommodate her customers who had made her place their official hangout, one of them offered that it would be nice if they had a dance floor there that would prevent the dirt from covering their shoes and socks as they danced to the music coming from their radios. Another friend agreed, and added, "Since Miss Dancie has the right name already, let's share our idea with her and see how she accepts it. Let's do it now before we lose our gumption."

Dancie had been able to constantly add to her nest egg because her business had been so successful. So when the teens approached her about a dance floor, she enthusiastically joined their excitement and thought it was a novel idea. Right away, Dancie began making plans to follow through with the teens' suggestion. She contacted Aunt Nell and asked again if she were willing to sell the property. And to her astonishment, Aunt Nell agreed to sell. One week after the sale was final, the foundation for a new addition to Dancie's Place was laid.

Dancie added a 40-by-40-foot dining-dancing hall to the existing structure. While it wasn't fancy, it was nice and functional. Around three walls Dancie added red vinyl restaurant booths with oak tables covered in red Formica. This provided maximum seating capacity for 64 customers, and a large dance floor in the center of the hall. Kids loved it because Dancie had a juke box installed with all the latest hits at their beck and call if they had a dime to spare. On the weekends, when the older crowd hung out at Buster's Place, teens had a hangout of their own—Dancie's Place. Parents did not hesitate to allow their teens to dine and dance at Dancie's on the weekend. They felt their children were safe there—and they were. It was a place for them to go to and have fun expending some of their pent-up energy, and everyone, not only from Hawk Town, but communities throughout Kinder County, loved it. The idea that had been born by teens now provided them their greatest enjoyment.

***

Granite Point Elementary School was completed mid-May and appointment letters sent out to all candidates who had been accepted for employment there. The new employees were to report for new employee orientation on Monday, June 1st. Joyce was the lucky recipient of one of the letters. She was bursting with excitement after opening the letter and learning her new employment status. She could hardly wait for Teddy to return from the trip he had taken to Silverboro that morning. She had so much she needed to do before June 1st, which was only two weeks away.

Joyce needed to shop for a few items of clothing that looked professional and suitable to be worn in the midst of school teachers even though she would be the administrative assistant. Parents and other adults visiting schools had high expectations of anyone interacting with children every day. So, Joyce wanted to be sure she would not be singled out for dressing inappropriately.

Everything had been running smoothly at home with Teddy and the three girls, and Joyce intended to keep it that way once she was engaged in full-time employment. Therefore, there were some tasks she needed to assign to Peggy, Annie, and Rosetta. Whereas Joyce had not heretofore put any pressure on the girls to help around the house, now that she would be away from home for eight hours every day, Monday through Friday, the girls had to be given more chores. Joyce would continue to do all the washing, shopping for and cooking meals, and heavy duty cleaning. But the girls would now have to assist with light cleaning—dusting and polishing furniture, cleaning windows, and sweeping all the floors and both porches daily. They were already rotating turns washing dishes. It was time to have a serious talk with them now, and she would discuss the changes with them tomorrow.

As soon as Teddy walked through the door that evening, Joyce greeted him with their usual kiss, and Teddy noticed she had one hand behind her back. He asked her what was she hiding, and Joyce showed him the letter, and he was happy, too. Even though he would have loved for Joyce not to work a full-time job outside their home, he was a practical guy and knew they could use the extra money. Taking care of three growing girls, and having to help his other siblings was expensive. But they had begun to manage well with Joyce working part time at Mt. Mercy Methodist Church and the Stapleton children receiving benefits after it was determined that they needed help since Clemis had disappeared without a trace.

Another deed Joyce needed to handle immediately was give notice that she would not be available at her church job after Friday, May 29th. She was glad that the appointment letter had arrived in time to allow her to give the church secretary an adequate notice, as two weeks was standard. Everything was working in Joyce and Teddy's favor at this point in their marriage.

On the first day of June, Joyce was one of the first excited individuals to arrive at the new school anxious to begin a new venture. Since she had gotten there early, Joyce found herself wandering down the hall and checking all the features that were state-of-the-art compared to the one-room school she had attended for 11 full years. Whereas the one-room school was an all wooden structure, this new school was a masterpiece of bricks and blocks. The halls, painted a light buff, were almost as wide as the whole school she had attended during her formative years. When she peeked in several classrooms, the walls were either pale green or very light blue in color. Everything emitted a fresh, new aroma. Joyce walked all the way to the end of the longest hall that terminated at the entrance to the gymtorium. The dual purpose of this enormous space would require a great deal of muscle power from the person or persons responsible for converting it to an auditorium for assemblies, and gym for physical activities, including all indoor sports events.

The room in which new staff orientation was scheduled to be held was at the opposite end of the building. It was a 20-by-30-foot room designed specifically to be used as a conference or training room with a counter across the entire width on one end, with storage space underneath. Bookcases lined the opposite end of the conference space. Two huge conference tables had been aligned so that 20 people could sit comfortably grouped together. When Joyce entered the conference room, she was greeted by a very attractive woman who appeared to be around 30 years old. She introduced herself as Miss Eva Robinson, the principal. Joyce introduced herself and said she had been hired to fill the position of administrative assistant. Miss Robinson told Joyce she was impressed by her punctuality. She said they were going to work well together and have a good first year in their brand-new school.

Everyone had been asked to report for orientation at 8:30 that morning. It was now 8:28 and it appeared that all the new staff was seated. Miss Robinson began by sharing her professional education background and experience with the assemblage. Then she asked everyone to share a brief synopsis of their background and how it relates to the position they would be filling at Granite Point Elementary School. There were two teachers for each grade—1 through 6—for a total of 12 classroom teachers. Each grade level would have two classrooms because students were going to be bused to Granite Point from communities throughout the southern half of Kinder County.

Additionally, the school had employed one librarian, two custodians, one administrative assistant, one music teacher, and three cafeteria staff. The custodians and cafeteria staff were not in attendance at this meeting because they had reported to the school a few days earlier and participated in a separate orientation arranged and designed exclusively for them.

The day's events progressed well. After classroom assignments were made, teachers began organizing their classrooms to their specific taste to accommodate new students in August. They had two months to prepare. During this time there had been a series of workshops designed to offer training for upgrading and enhancing their skills. There were also workshops for reviewing some aspects of Child and Adolescent Psychology, as well as Strategies for Dealing with Difficult people, and Building Rapport with Colleagues. This new principal, Miss Robinson, was leaving no stone unturned. She had arranged a full schedule of summer activities for her staff.

***

The new bridge on Highway 102 opened on June 20th, just in time to handle the upcoming holiday traffic. People would be headed to Bottomsail Beach and this was the route most visitors to the area traveled to get to the beach. Independence Day celebrations generated gala affairs of family and friends. There was always a multitude of activities—family reunions, cookouts, dances, and parties galore. Hawk Town residents even had an annual school reunion. This year it would be held at the fabulous new Granite Point Elementary School that had opened its doors for staff orientation and training one month prior to the grand event of which everyone was excited about. However, the school would not hold open house to showcase for taxpayers the bargain they were getting for supporting education projects until the Friday before August 1st.

Completion of the bridge and the school meant the area would be losing population because men who had come to the area solely for construction purposes would now be returning home or moving on to complete other projects. So, that was another cause for celebrations. Old acquaintances and new friendships that had amalgamated were sharing a kaleidoscope of emotions. In the midst of all the rumpus, both Buster's Place and Miss Circe's Place were overflowing with business. The atmosphere was synonymous to a last hurrah. Granite Point and Hawk Town had not seen this much fanfare since the two towns celebrated the end of World War II.

While it appeared for months, especially the months following Clemis' disappearance, that Cora was too busy to establish a relationship with a fellow, secretly she had been dating Thomas Hickson, the foreman of laborers for the bridge construction. She and Tom, as she called him, had been dating for eight months and their courtship had progressed beyond the point of no return, as far as they both were concerned. Now the time had come to make a major decision.

Tom knew in his heart that Cora was the woman that he wanted in his world for a lifetime. But he understood her commitment to her family and was willing to share her, up to a point, until Daisy had completed studying a year at Dillington College. He had not had this discussion with Cora and was apprehensive about his approach for broaching the subject. He could no longer delay this discussion with Cora because in two weeks he would be moving on to Clemmetsville, which was 400 miles north of Hawk Town. Tom was experiencing varying degrees of emotions. His strongest inclination was to propose to Cora and to prepare himself to accept the fact that she might say, "No." He felt that in order to propose, he needed to have a ring to offer her. If she did not accept it, he could always return it before he left the area. He had time and his decision was made. Tomorrow he would purchase an engagement ring.

When Tom and Cora met for their usual Friday night date, Tom was emboldened and he didn't waste any time. He removed the ring from his pocket and asked Cora to be his wife. For a few moments she was speechless. During those few moments Tom was feeling so much angst that he thought he would disintegrate before she answered. With a quavering voice, Cora, after what seemed like a lifetime to Tom, said, "Yes." She could not believe her dream had come true. It was the most beautiful ring she had ever seen, and it fit her finger perfectly. Cora had been lamenting the fact that Tom would be leaving and she might never see him again, and now she knew she had been dithery unnecessarily. At the moment she was weakened by sheer joy, so much so that she was temporarily immobilized. All she could do was close her eyes and fall achingly into Tom's arms. They sat quietly holding each other for a long time. Words were not necessary. There were no words that could accurately capture what they both were feeling.

Tom told Cora that he had no expectations of taking her away from her family at this time. He said they could marry in a private ceremony before a justice of the peace, and she could stay in Hawk Town until he was more settled in Clemmetsville. He said he would come to Hawk Town on weekends. It was a six-hour drive from Clemmetsville to Hawk Town. Tom would leave at noon on Fridays and arrive in Hawk Town by 6 o'clock, and he would leave Hawk Town at noon on Sundays for the return trip to Clemmetsville. Tom said he would lease one of the three suites that Miss Circe had converted from her three-car garage so that he and Cora would have some privacy on the weekends when he came to Hawk Town. They would only need to keep this arrangement for six months because by that time Daisy would have completed the school year and would be in a position to take charge more and manage the Stapleton household. Having Teddy and Joyce living within earshot allayed any fears that might otherwise cause Daisy any doubts in terms of having support when she needed it.

It was a long, hot and languorous summer; the average outdoor temperature was 95 degrees. Kids would be spending more time participating in indoor activities when school opened in a few weeks. The heat would prohibit their spending too much time outdoors. Yet and still, everyone was excited about the upcoming school year. Joyce's excitement was as pizzazzy as the school-age kids. She was elated over having the opportunity to participate in the educational workshops and training that Miss Robinson had arranged for staff.

Summer was steamrolling rapidly toward the beginning of the new school year. Open House of the new Granite Point Elementary School was just around the corner. August was only two weeks away.

Miss Robinson and her staff were winding down as the last of the summer's workshops would end on

Friday. That would leave one week to plan copiously for Open House, which was scheduled on Friday, July 29th. The new school year would officially begin on Monday, August 1st.

Teachers had completed all necessary operations in their classrooms. Bulletin boards were decorated appropriately for each grade level, seat assignments had been graphically blocked and posted inside the teachers' desk to quickly enable them to associate names with faces. All books and supplies were in place, and there was nothing left to do inside the classrooms except wait to receive the happy faces next Monday.

During the week staff would be decorating halls, receiving plants donated by Stowe's Nursery to add aesthetics to the already attractive building, and placing them strategically throughout the building in areas that did not receive as much student traffic daily. Three local grocery stores were donating all the ingredients necessary for the makings of lemonade, iced tea, and fruit punch. Those items would be brought to the school on Thursday to be refrigerated after the proper ingredients and finishing touches were in the mix, to be cold for the function on Friday. Cakes and cookies being donated would be received Friday morning.

Officials, parents and children, and interested parties from around Kinder County would be in attendance at this event. After time had been allowed for everyone to wander through the new school building, time has been set aside for a 45-minute interactive program whereby the superintendent of schools would provide a brief overview of what parents and the community could expect throughout the school year; and thereafter parents and other interested parties would be given the opportunity to ask questions. A school directory that included the calendar for the year, attendance requirements, disciplinary procedures, and lunch and cafeteria policies would be disseminated at the close of the program. The reception was scheduled to end at 7 o'clock Friday evening. It would be the end of a long day for Miss Robinson and her staff, but they would have the weekend to recuperate and hopefully be eager to begin work Monday morning.

On the afternoon of Open House, one would have thought it was the 4th of July all over again. People from the farthest corners of Kinder County had come to get an up close and personal look at the new school. From the town of Anderson on the westernmost corner to the town of Bottomsail on the easternmost corner, and from the town of Hilliston in the northern section of the county, they all came. There was not an empty space in the school's parking lot, and cars lined both sides of the road for a quarter mile in both directions. Friends who had not seen each other in years used this time to socialize and play catch-up on happenings of years past. And in some instances, new friendships were formed. Open House for this new school was a joyous occasion—one that would be remembered indelibly for years to come.

When everyone had seen the school building's finest features and had settled in the gymtorium, Miss Robinson stood at the podium, begged everyone's attention, and re-introduced herself. She called upon Rev. Herman to open the assembly with a prayer. Afterward, she introduced Kinder County School Superintendent Mr. Kenneth Monroe, who was pleased with the turnout, and he described it as one of epic proportion for an open-house event. He promised a productive school year and an open mind and open door should there be any occurrences throughout the year that warranted his special attention beyond the routine responsibilities of the job.

As the superintendent was speaking, John Riverbank, who was in attendance with a group from Anderson, his hometown, appeared to have been mesmerized as he sat staring at Miss Robinson. He was not tuned in to a word Mr. Monroe was saying; he was absorbed in thoughts of wanting to introduce himself to the new principal. John had not dated anyone since his return to the South. Actually, he has been so busy that he had not had time to even consider dating. He had not been anywhere in particular to meet anyone he would have liked to date—hadn't given dating a second thought—until now. Before he left the school this evening, he would find a way to approach the principal, introduce himself, and hope to ingratiate himself into a corner of her mind. He realized that there was a world of new people she was meeting for the first time this evening, but he was going to hang around to be sure he was one of the last attendees to leave the school at 7 o'clock.

Although she gave no indication, Miss Robinson did not miss the sight of John Riverbank staring at her. She had noticed him, too, but she was careful not to get caught staring at him. She was wondering if he had children who would be attending Granite Point Elementary. She could see he was not wearing a wedding band—but lots of married men don't. She also noticed that he did not appear to be escorting a female this evening. She decided she would casually ask Joyce about him later this evening or Monday morning. She realized her thoughts had drifted and consciously brought her attention back to the meeting and business at hand.

As the evening wore on and all speeches made, Miss Robinson asked everyone to stop by the tables in the hallway and take a school directory that included, among other items of interest, phone numbers that would put them in touch with school personnel when necessary. As she was giving instructions, John was still trying to think of a pertinent question to ask her on his way out. He knew elementary students were too young to know very much, if anything, about forensic medicine and forensic psychology, or pathology. But he was going to find a reason to somehow make himself available to the school and Miss Robinson. He would think of something.

John lingered in the hall just outside the gymtorium and pretended to be studying one of the decorated bulletin boards that displayed a floor plan of the school that indicated where all exists were located. He waited until Miss Robinson was exiting the gymtorium and approached her in a gentlemanly fashion. He stated his name and told her he was impressed with her plans for the school. Miss Robinson seemed pleasantly surprised about the comment and she thanked John for being there.

"What brings a coroner to the school's Open House?" she inquired politely. "Do you have children who will be attending school here?"

"No," John replied. "I am a single coroner interested in helping the school and community any way that I can. I realize that my profession is of little or no interest to kids in elementary school, but perhaps when you hold Career Day or some other event where professionals are invited to come and share information about their work status in life, you will consider inviting me. We never know what interest kids that age might find in what I do in the larger scheme of life."

Miss Robinson told John he was absolutely correct. She asked if he had a card she could keep, and John could not remove a card from his pocket quickly enough. What John didn't know was that when they had this brief interlude in the hall, Miss Robinson already knew who he was because she had spotted him before the program began and had asked Joyce who the handsome guy was wearing the light blue shirt, khaki pants, and Dockers. John thanked Miss Robinson again for her service to the community, and she was pleased that they had become acquainted. She planned to contact him the first time she could cleverly arrange an activity that would give her an excuse to do so. John bid Miss Robinson good evening and left the school floating on cloud nine.

***

All too soon for some, and not soon enough for others, the first day of school was here. Teachers had arrived early in order to be in place when their first students reported for class. Not to be outdone, Joyce arrived early as well, and was in the office sorting programs for the assembly that was scheduled to begin in one hour. The morning was aflutter with enthusiasm. Throughout the day, activities were orchestrated according to plan and when it was time to dismiss students in the afternoon, the overriding consensus was it had been a near perfect first day.

Months rolled by and the school year was running smoothly. Joyce was a punctilious administrative assistant. She kept schedules and plans for the school orderly for Miss Robinson. Thus far, Joyce had perfect attendance.

During the month of December while school was closed for Christmas vacation, Joyce began feeling listless, lacking the exhilaration usually seen in her during this special time of year. Teddy noticed her doldrums and thought she might be having symptoms of a cold or flu, but she was not feverish and did not have a cough. After several days, he asked Joyce if she needed to see their family physician, Dr. Fox, who actually was everyone in Hawk Town's family physician because he was the only doctor around for miles. Because Joyce was feeling weak and lackadaisical, she said that might be a good idea. It was the 19th day of December when Joyce made the appointment, and Dr. Fox had to stay late in the evening on December 20th to see Joyce because he had no vacant slots during regular office hours this close to Christmas. It was the anniversary of their wedding reception one year ago.

At 6:30 on the evening on December 20th, Joyce was waiting in Dr. Fox's office. After he had seen his last patient, he was ready to examine Joyce. When Dr. Fox had finished checking all of her vital signs, which were normal, he asked Joyce when she had had her last monthly cycle. Joyce instantly knew why the question had been asked. While she had not thought about it beforehand, because she had been so busy, she had not had a period since October. Being busy at school, and the celebration with family during Thanksgiving, she had not thought about the fact that she had missed a period in November.   Since more than half the month of December had passed, it meant that by now she had missed two periods.   With a smile, Dr. Fox offered congratulations.   Joyce and Teddy were going to be parents of their very own son or daughter.

When Joyce walked through the front door of their home, Teddy was waiting anxiously to hear the results of Dr. Fox's diagnosis and prognosis.   Joyce, although feeling exhausted from the trip to the doctor, was all smiles.   She asked Teddy to sit with her in the living room, took his hand and led him to the sofa.   Once they were seated she looked directly at him and said, "You're going to be a father."   Teddy was ecstatic.   He stood up and shouted, "I'm going to be a father!"   His spirits were lifted so high that he felt the need to celebrate.   He told Joyce not to bother making dinner. He was going to spoil the family this evening with one of Miss Dancie's good ole home-cooked meals.   He would have the opportunity to share their good news with Miss Dancie and the guys at Buster's Place.   He hugged and kissed Joyce, then dashed out the door to order dinner for them.   When Teddy returned, he brought back fried chicken, rice and gravy, macaroni and cheese, collard greens, corn muffins, and apple pie for dessert.   The girls would have iced tea and he and Joyce would have a glass of Clemis' finest wine.

While Joyce and the girls were setting the table, Teddy went out to the shed on their new property and brought back wine made from scuppernong grapes. As they sat down around the dinner table, they each took turns offering a blessing and thanking God for bringing a new life into the Stapleton Family.

There is always extra ardor in the air during the Christmas holidays. And even though Joyce was feeling sluggish and sleeping more than she normally did, she was radiant and happy and excited to have several weeks of vacation to relax and enjoy the seasonal activity. It was the season of joy, and she had more than her share of happiness knowing that she and Teddy were having a child. She was not anxious about the sex of the child-- boy or girl—it didn't matter. She only prayed that their child would be healthy and wholesome, and she thanked God for this special gift. It was a great Christmas gift for both Teddy and her. They didn't need anything else this Christmas. They would appreciate the gift exchange among the family, but nothing could compare in magnitude to the gift of the new life they were expecting. It would be fair to say that after receiving news that they were expecting, Joyce and Teddy were overjoyed beyond measure this holiday season.

Teddy was like a kid who had received his ultimate wish from Santa Claus. He was all smiles—cheerful, playful, and lighthearted. He told Joyce he wanted to buy Christmas gifts for the baby instead of spending money on gifts for himself this year. Teddy had always been a conservative when it came to spending, and Joyce was delighted to know that already he was willing to spoil their baby with gifts. Yet she cautioned him earnestly about spoiling a child.

Joyce, sensible as usual, asked Teddy to wait before shopping for their unborn child. She reminded him that it would be almost seven more months before the baby was born, which gave them more than enough time to convert the guest room into a nursery and purchase small items they felt would be needed for a newborn. As sweetly as she could, she asked Teddy to quiet the storm of his excitement. And they both laughed and hugged each other tenderly.

Teddy said to Joyce that if she felt up to taking a short ride, tomorrow they would go and share their good news with Miss Circe after they had stopped by his family home and shared the wonderful expectation with all of his siblings. They would take the girls along so they could hear the news at the same time as the rest of the family.

The holidays were over all too soon. The New Year celebrations had been as effusive and illustrious as ever. There had been parties and fireworks throughout small towns and villages identical to those celebrations in larger cities. Families were hopeful that the New Year would bring continuous prosperity and good will. As do all merrymaking periods and events, there comes a time when it must end and the slight detour they bring in the course of life must return to its normal cycle. Hawk Town and Granite Point were no exception.

**

It was back to business as usual when everyone returned to school on January 2nd. Kids were eager to share their holiday experiences with friends and, of course, talk about the gifts they received and, in the case of the little ones, tell what Santa had brought them. Faculty and staff shared some of their holiday experiences as well.

Miss Robinson noticed that Joyce was not as active as she would have expected her to be. Joyce normally would have been talking more and sharing news relative to her family's activities during the holiday season as she had done following Thanksgiving. But Joyce was unusually quiet—so much so that when they were alone in the office, Miss Robinson asked Joyce if everything was OK. Joyce's face immediately beamed radiantly as she faced Miss Robinson and smiled. Excitedly, Joyce answered, "Teddy and I are expecting!" Then Joyce shared that she had not been as energetic as usual during the holidays, so Teddy became concerned and suggested that she let Dr. Fox take a look at her. And she did because she was thinking maybe her sluggishness was due to the onset of a cold or virus, even though she wasn't feverish. But as it turned out, after the examination, Dr. Fox announced that she was pregnant. Miss Robinson was overcome by exuberance as Joyce shared her good news. She felt this was one more element of joy they could look forward to this New Year as they plowed through the second half of the school year together.

Politely, Joyce then asked Miss Robinson how she had spent her vacation. The principal said she had gone home to Charleston, S.C., to visit her family. She stayed with her parents where all of her siblings and their families gathered for dinner on Christmas Eve, Christmas Day, New Year's Eve, and New Year's Day. She said this had been as family tradition for as long as she could remember. Miss Robinson said throughout the holidays her family did so many fun things together. They looked through old photo albums and reminisced about days gone by. She shared childhood stories with her brothers and sisters and they matched her stories with memories of their own; and all of the adults devoted time to the children—taking them to visit Santa, shopping and exchanging gifts, and dining at their favorite local restaurants. They simply spent time together making more good memories. Finally, she said that even though she had thoroughly enjoyed the time with her family, she had been eager to return to Xenolina, most especially to Granite Point Elementary School.

And speaking of the usual school business, Miss Robinson shared with Joyce that she would like to arrange a Career Day program for 5th and 6th grades during the month of February. She said as the school would be celebrating Black History Month, it would be an ideal time to bring professionals of all races together in a forum where students could listen to them give details about their various professions and entertain any questions student might have. Miss Robinson asked Joyce's opinion of what she was planning, and Joyce said she thought it was a great idea.

Miss Robinson said over the weekend she had developed a list of the professions and careers that she felt would be of interest to young aspiring minds, and she asked Joyce to be prepared to send out invitations to each of the professions she had chosen by the end of the week. This being the first week in January only gave them a few weeks to put together a complete action plan.

Miss Robinson would draft the invitation and have it ready for Joyce to type by Wednesday. Joyce would immediately begin to address all envelopes and construct a list of telephone numbers of everyone on Miss Robinson's invitation list. Letters would be mailed out on Friday. Once the letters had been mailed, Miss Robinson would wait two weeks and then follow up with a telephone call. When it has been determined how many speakers would participate, Joyce would finalize the scheduled line-up of speakers in accordance with Miss Robinson's instructions.

Joyce could have no way of knowing how anxious Miss Robinson was to see John Riverbank again. She had thought about him off and on all during the Christmas holidays. And she began to plan a Career Day program to be held during the month of February, primarily because she wanted to communicate with John again face-to-face. Ordinarily, Career Day would be scheduled during the month of April, but Eva felt she could not wait that long to see John again. She wondered what was happening to her because she had never felt an attraction this strong for anyone, ever! She wondered if it would be too forward if she penned a few personal words in the invitation going out to John. She would think about it. She had until Friday to decide.

As the school year advanced and winter faded into spring, Joyce began to feel much better in the second trimester of her pregnancy, and it became apparent to everyone that she was carrying a child. As time drew nearer Joyce's delivery date, her co-workers at school, family and friends at Mt. Mercy Methodist Church, and folks in the community anxiously awaited the baby's debut.

At home, the nursery had been decorated with pastel pink, blue, yellow, and green alphabets and nursery rhymes. Joyce had decided to leave the walls the mint green color since they did not know if their baby would be a boy or girl. They played a variety of guessing games about how to determine the sex of an unborn child, but it was all just fun and games. No one took stock in those predictions. Even the Ouija board forecast was dismissed. Teddy had not been able to resist purchasing teddy bears of all sizes. They added a precious touch to the nursery. There was nothing left to do now but wait.

PART IV

Natalie Perkins was quiet, seemingly subdued, and often seen staring into space—totally disconnected from her surroundings. By this time, Daisy Stapleton was in college. Natalie sat next to Daisy in class and periodically she would step back into reality briefly to ask what the professor had just said. After writing a few concise notes, Natalie would drift back into her private world. The class was small—only seven students in the evening Education 601 class at Dillington College. Natalie was the oldest student in the class. It wasn't long before the students had bonded into a close-knit group. They studied together and sometimes met for an early dinner before class begun. In the restaurants they chose, people were lively, carefree, and unconcerned about their present surroundings, but Natalie was distant. Sometimes a member of the group would make a conscious effort to draw her into the conversation; but most of the time she floated on another cloud—not really concerned with anything or anybody in her present company.

Natalie had married as soon as she graduated high school and was unable to begin a college education at that time because she was pregnant, and Charlie, her sometimes sexual partner, felt that it was his duty to marry her immediately after she told him that she was carrying his child. He and Natalie were not in love with each other and never pretended to be. They simply enjoyed mating. They were polite and respectful of each other. To have seen them together, one would have thought that they were deeply in love. Outwardly, they presented a façade of being mesmerized with one another.

Charlie had actually begun to despise Natalie not long after they were married. Not because of anything she had or had not done, but because he was hopelessly engrossed with the idea of a life with Patricia Bailey, daughter of Joe Bailey, one of the wealthiest men in neighboring Rublin County. Charlie had plans to marry Patricia, mostly because he had his eyes and hopes set on one day inheriting Joe Bailey's lucrative cattle business and the money that came along with it. Charlie wasn't too fond of farming. As a matter of fact, he loathed the idea. But he would fake any actions necessary to impress his future father-in-law that his daughter was landing a fine catch in Charlie Pittman.

Patricia Bailey was deeply in love with Charlie Pittman. He was eight years older than she was, and had completed four years of college already. He was tall, lean, blond, and blue-eyed. He had been a track star in high school and college, and at one time had had hopes for competing in the Olympics. But an auto accident his junior year of college had left him with a bum knee. One would never notice it just by observing him because he was fortunate enough not to be cursed with a limp. But Charlie knew his success on the track was overdue to the excruciating pain he felt in his knee from time to time.

Patricia was young, beautiful, vivacious, cultured, and energetic. Charlie loved everything about her and knew deep down in his soul that she would be the perfect wife for a budding politician. Because while Charlie had never told anyone about his dreams for his future, his greatest desire was to one day become a state senator. His Uncle Dan had been a senator when Charlie was a young boy, and Charlie had never forgotten all of the attention that was emblazoned on his uncle. Charlie loved attention and he had gotten more than enough as a high school and college track star. But Charlie knew he would not be young forever, and in the recesses of his mind, his fixation was on one day becoming a state senator. Charlie also knew that Patricia's class and charisma, and her daddy's money, would pave a sure way for him to reach his ultimate goal.

Patricia had no idea that, even though he cared for her, Charlie was actually clamoring to use her and her daddy's wealth to fill the void of his exiguous position. Even though Charlie was still a star of sorts in the eyes of the public, he had come from humble beginnings. His father, before he retired, was a blue-collar worker at the only large industry in Rublin County. His mother owned a beauty boutique, and as a small business owner, had lived through many struggles over the years. But both of his parents were honest, hard-working individuals. And in the rural South, people respected that.

Because Patricia was a cultured young lady with a Christian upbringing, she had never given in to Charlie's pressure to have sex with him. And because Charlie respected and cared so much for her, he could wait until she was ready. But in the meantime, Charlie was enjoying sexual escapades with the young girls who were willing partners. And it just so happened that he had gotten careless with Natalie Perkins, and consequently had felt he had to marry her. In his mind, Patricia was young and naïve. And even though he felt she would be devastated over the news that he had to marry Natalie, he felt he could convince her that she was the only true love of his life and they could wait a few years until he could give his unborn child a proper name, and then get a divorce. He would tell Patricia that in a few years she will have finished college and would be ready for marriage.

When Natalie had learned she was pregnant, she had been devastated. She knew she would have to abandon her plans to attend college immediately after her high school graduation. But while that saddened her, nothing compared to the pain she felt over having to tell her parents. She was so ashamed and was overcome with a feeling of desolation. She wondered what was going to happen to her. She was worried that her parents might ask her to leave home and she had no place to go, very little money saved, no means of providing for herself and a baby, nothing!

After pondering her situation a few days, Natalie decided that her first best move would be to break the terrible news to Charlie and see if he would be willing to help her. She did not deceive herself into any expectation of marriage. And she told Charlie the very next evening when they met at their usual spot by the river. Charlie was totally perturbed by the news. There was a long pause with no conversation between the two of them for several minutes. Charlie had laid his head back against the rear window of his pickup truck, closed his eyes, and taken deep lung-filling breaths, while

Natalie sat nervously holding her breath waiting for him to confront her.

Finally, Charlie turned toward Natalie and opened his eyes. His first words were, "It's going to be OK. I am so sorry I did this to you." And he took Natalie into his arms as a river of tears fell from her eyes. They remained embraced for quite a while. And then Natalie broke away and asked Charlie, "What are we going to do?" Charlie asked if she were willing to marry him. And she said there was nothing that could please her more. Natalie was so relieved. All of the tension that had been welled up in her since she first learned she was pregnant, suddenly was released as she continued to cry, but with tears of joy. Charlie told her that on the following evening he would come to the Perkinses' home and ask Mr. and Mrs. Perkins for her hand in marriage. And then he decided it was time for Natalie to go home, and he needed time to think.

On the drive back to her home, Natalie had a rapid succession of thoughts bundling in her head, the most prevalent being, "What was Charlie going to do about Patricia?" Because it was understood by all of their friends and acquaintances that Charlie and Patricia, even with the difference in their ages, were a couple.

By the time she was turning into the driveway of her home, Natalie had abandoned all thoughts except how her situation had been radically altered in a matter of several hours. Her mood had changed from worry and depression to euphoria. She definitely wanted to be able to keep her baby. The thought of adoption had sickened her, and abortion would never be an option as far as she was concerned. Charlie's quick decision about marriage elevated him to a brighter light in their relationship. But she wondered if he would have second thoughts later on and would fail to show at her home the next evening as he had promised. It was a scary thought.

The following evening Charlie paid a visit to the Perkinses' residence as promised. Mr. and Mrs. Perkins had finished dinner and were relaxing in their den when Charlie knocked at their front door. Because they weren't expecting any visitors, and door-to-door salesmen did not usually come around at this hour, they wondered who it could be. Mr. Perkins got up and went to the door. He opened the door without asking who was there. He was surprised to see Charlie Pittman, the superstar from high school and college. Mr. Perkins had not seen Charlie in years. He greeted Charlie quite pleasantly and asked Charlie what had brought him to their home this evening, and invited Charlie to come in, all in the same breath. Mr. Pittman invited Charlie to have a seat.

When Charlie sat nervously, he said he was there to see them about Natalie. Back in the kitchen, Natalie had heard Charlie speaking with her parents, so she stopped what she was doing and joined them. She spoke to Charlie and fell silent. She remained standing. Charlie stated to Natalie's parents that he was sure they were unaware that he and Natalie had been dating for quite some time. Both Mr. and Mrs. Perkins were surprised at that bit of news.

Mr. Perkins said to Charlie, "Aren't you about to marry Joe Bailey's daughter as soon as she finishes her schooling? Everybody knows that's your young girlfriend. Aren't the two of you engaged?" Mr. Perkins went on to say that Joe Bailey was his boss and he had been working for him for more than 25 years, and he did not want any trouble from his boss because of Charlie's fooling around with Natalie. And he said, "To answer your question—No! My wife and I were not aware that you and Natalie have been seeing each other!"

Mr. Perkins then looked at Natalie quizzically and said, "So you have been sneaking around in the dark with a man who intends to marry another woman, huh? What does that make you?"

Olivia Perkins interrupted and said, "Hush, David! Don't speak to Natalie that way! Let this young man tell us why he came here this evening."

Charlie then said he had come to ask for Natalie's hand in marriage, and Natalie's parents were shocked.

Mr. Perkins said, "I can't believe what I'm hearing! What's going on?"

Natalie spoke up and said, "I'm pregnant, Mom and Dad." Both of her parents were devastated—and speechless.

Charlie continued by telling David and Olivia Perkins that he wanted to do the right thing, and he would take good care of Natalie and the child they were expecting.

Mr. Perkins said, "That's mighty noble of you, son, but what about Joe Bailey's daughter? Where does she fit in this fiasco?"

Charlie told the Perkins that he was going to inform Patricia right away, but he needed to get beyond this first step of informing them and seeking their approval before speaking with Patricia.

Mr. Perkins said, "I feel sorry for you, young man, because if I know Joe Bailey, he is not going to take it lightly that you are humiliating his daughter."

During this entire exchange, Natalie stood silently with tears streaming down her face. Olivia Perkins got up, went to her daughter, and embraced her tenderly.

Charlie and Natalie appeared before a justice of the peace the following Thursday and were married in a quiet ceremony with Natalie's parents as the only witnesses. The Perkinses only solace was that their daughter would not suffer this embarrassment alone. They were appreciative of Charlie's attempt to prevent their daughter from spiraling further in the wrong direction.

***

Four years have passed since Charlie made the decision to marry Natalie. The restlessness he has felt ever since he said, "I do," has been overbearing to the point that he wants out of the marriage, now. The primary reason, above many other reasons, is that Patricia Bailey, the woman he desires, is now one month from becoming a college graduate. Ironically, his wife, Natalie, has just enrolled as a college freshman. Charlie's life is more complicated than he had ever imagined. Four years ago he felt that when the time was ripe, he would simply ask Natalie for a divorce. He had felt at the time that she would not contest the divorce because, after all, he had done her a favor by marrying her. Moreover, he had never really bonded with their 3½-year- old daughter because somehow he had managed to be an absentee dad even though they all lived under the same roof. Charlie was away a great deal of the time because he worked as an insurance adjuster— a job that kept him on the go. He was extremely busy during and following hurricane season, because southeastern Xenolina seemed to have been a magnet for hurricane strikes that caused massive destruction.

Being away from home so often had given Charlie time to rendezvous secretly with Patricia at the university she was attending since it was 200 miles from Kinder County and no one knew that Charlie was Patricia's paramour. Many of Patricia's friends thought that Charlie was Patricia's older brother. He would come to campus and take Patricia to dinner, or shopping, or a movie, so her friends thought they were relatives. But those long hours away from campus, when her friends thought Patricia was at a movie, were actually spent at a motel with Charlie, and they weren't having dinner either—they were having sex.

Charlie had finally been gifted with the opportunity of stealing Patricia's virginity. Over time, Patricia had begun to desire Charlie so much that she could no longer fight his sexual advances. When she gave in to him the first time, it was ecstasy beyond anything she had ever imagined. And after that first time, there was no turning back. She longed to be in Charlie's arms and to feel him inside of her as much as Charlie desired to be with her. When Patricia knew Charlie was coming for a visit, she could not concentrate on her studies. And she loved it even more when Charlie paid her a surprise visit.

So for four years Charlie had committed adultery with Patricia, and Patricia had been drowning with desire for him, and anticipating the day when she would become Mrs. Charlie Pittman. As time grew closer and closer to graduation, she had begun to pressure Charlie about initiating steps towards divorcing Natalie. And Charlie was feeling the pressure. He began to weigh other options for getting out of his marriage as alternatives to divorce. Primarily, he was thinking about the financial aspects of divorcing Natalie. He knew he would have to give her their home and he would have to continue paying the mortgage, taxes, and insurance. He also knew that he and Natalie had meager savings in the bank, but nothing else—no stocks or bonds or other property.

One thing that had kept resonating in Charlie's mind was that he and Natalie had a million-dollar insurance on each other. He was thinking how far a million dollars could help him advance the new plans he had for himself. Having a little nest egg would, hopefully, be impressive to Patricia and her father. Otherwise, he would be entering the marriage as a pauper. And Charlie felt there was no way he was going to begin his new life with nothing of substance to offer a new wife. So he was leaning strongly toward getting rid of Natalie in the worst way. As much as he dreaded the thought of his little girl being without her mother for the rest of her life, the thought of his being without Patricia and her daddy's money for the rest of his life was bleaker. After all, he felt strongly that Natalie's mother would be a good substitute mother in his daughter's life. It was her beloved grandchild—her only grandchild.

As Charlie was making his plans, Natalie was feeling it. Her extrasensory perception and mental telepathy were operating in overdrive. She had felt all during the four years of their marriage that Charlie was having an affair. But she could never find any proof of her suspicions. So she never really dwelled on the idea, but she was not oblivious to the fact that he had many opportunities to do so, and she and Charlie, although married and parents, were never that close. And lately she was beginning to see signs that Charlie might be planning her demise. And this is what pushed her to the brink to the point that she began numbing herself with prescription medication.

Natalie had confided in her family physician that she was feeling extremely stressed and needed a mild tranquilizer. What, with a 3-year-old in child day care, and her entering college for the first time at her age, in addition to the fact that Charlie was away from home a great deal of the time, leaving her to care for their daughter single-handedly. It was no wonder Natalie felt that she was about to become unglued. So her physician had prescribed for Natalie a 90-day supply of Prozac.

As life became more complicated now that she was attending classes, Natalie began to medicate herself more and more. While the prescribed instructions stated that Natalie should take only one dose per day as needed, Natalie was taking two, sometimes three pills per day. And that is one of the reasons why Natalie often slept in class. And when she wasn't sleeping, she appeared to be dazed and distant, presenting the appearance of someone who was highly intoxicated. However, she had begun to feel a closeness to Daisy Stapleton and during class one evening, out of the blue, she shocked Daisy by turning to her and pleading, "You've got to help me. Please, they are going to kill me." Daisy didn't know what to say. Natalie then looked at Daisy with a lack of recognition and resumed her usual posture of staring into space.

Daisy assumed, of course, that Natalie was hallucinating. Daisy felt that Natalie was rambling aimlessly through a figment of her imagination. Yet Daisy was curious and needed to know for herself whether or not Natalie's imagination was causing the feelings she was expressing, or if this was a real circumstance. So Daisy asked Natalie who was going to kill her, and Natalie replied, "My husband." Daisy felt that was the most ridiculous idea she had heard in a long time. Almost everyone in Kinder County who knew Charlie Pittman felt he was an honorable family man who appeared to adore his wife and beautiful little daughter. He was friendly, outgoing and engaging, with a personality that heightened his ability to make insurance adjustments with the least amount of friction. Daisy felt it was prudent to dismiss Natalie's accusation as a fabrication. She was thinking that Natalie had a vivid imagination. However, the thought of what Natalie was claiming had not completely paled into insignificance with Daisy because when she got home from school that evening she mentioned Natalie's accusation to her eldest sister, Cora, who was still living at home and in charge of the Stapleton household.

Cora replied, "She's probably hallucinating. Because from the description you have given of her in the past, I would guess that she is a heavy drug user—albeit prescription drugs." Cora warned Daisy not to ever mention to anyone else this particular conversation she had had with Natalie. Cora reminded her, as if she needed to, that Natalie and Charlie were white and that was a serious charge for a black woman to level against a white man, even if it were hearsay. And what if Natalie was making it up? Or what if Natalie would deny ever having said it because she was in a drunken stupor when the words were spoken from the recesses of her mind, and later on she truly could not remember having made a claim of that nature? Where would that leave Daisy? And Daisy would be the one to have earned a reputation as a liar in everyone's minds. Daisy understood and promised never to repeat the story again.

Two nights after Daisy had listened to Natalie's accusations and dreadful prediction, Natalie did not show up for class and had not mentioned during the previous class that she would miss class Wednesday night. As a rule, when she, or any of the other six students had to be absent, they would let another member of the class, or the professor know, if they knew, in advance. As a rule, Natalie would have let Daisy, if no one else, know that she had to miss class Wednesday evening.

When Daisy arrived home after class that Wednesday night, Cora met her on the porch. "Did you hear what happened to Natalie?" she asked. Daisy was dumbfounded by the question. "No, what happened to her?" Cora told Daisy that she heard that Natalie had fallen down the stairs in her home and had broken her neck. Daisy asked Cora how was Natalie doing, and Cora let her know that Natalie was dead.

Daisy was suddenly weak in her knees and overcome by an indescribable sense of dread. Thoughts were dancing in her head that Natalie had appealed to her for help and she had failed her. But how was she to know? And maybe it was an accident. After all, lately Natalie always appeared to be under the influence of some intoxicating substance. Could Charlie have pushed her down the stairs, carrying out the prediction that Natalie had made? She didn't want to think about it. Yet she could not deny that it was a strong possibility that that is exactly what had happened. And Cora was having similar thoughts about the situation, too. She was thinking that perhaps she had given Daisy the wrong advice. Maybe she had jumped to the wrong conclusion too quickly. But how was she to know? She was thinking only of Daisy and the fact that she did not want Daisy to get caught up in a tangled web of deception and lies and lose her reputation as a nice Christian young lady. She thought, "Oh, my God! What had she done? Could she and Daisy have prevented this death?" They would never know.

The only recourse for Daisy and Cora now was to keep silent about Natalie's appeal to Daisy for help. The two sisters were in an uncomfortable position. If they said anything now, who would believe them? They knew Natalie and Charlie had a daughter whom Charlie would now have to care for. So why make trouble for Charlie on only a supposition that Natalie might have been telling the truth? All aspects of the situation considered, they knew it would be best to keep silent. It would be their secret.

***

In recent years, Charlie knew that Natalie had earned a reputation as a lush, because there was not much distinction between a drunk and a doper in terms of their behavior and appearances. No one would suspect that he had pushed her down the stairs—which he had, but only to camouflage the fact that he had broken her neck beforehand, and she was already dead when he pushed her to the bottom of the stairs.

When Natalie woke up and was getting out of bed on Wednesday, after having slept until 11 o'clock, he had reminded her that in 30 more minutes it would be time to pick up their daughter from the child day care center. He also reminded Natalie that he had a 12 noon appointment to meet a farmer who had lost some cattle when Stony Creek had flooded during recent heavy rains, and the cattle had been trapped in the creek's flood waters and had drowned. He stated emphatically that she needed to get a move on and be ready to arrive at the center on time because there were extra charges added to the already astronomical fees when a caretaker or parent was late for pickup, and he and Natalie were not exactly flushed with cash to spare. As a matter of fact, now that

Natalie was enrolled in college and attending classes in the evening, their budget had been tighter than ever before during the four years of their marriage.

In what had become her usual vitriolic fashion, Natalie had snapped back at him that she didn't feel up to going to the center today, and Charlie was just going to have to make time in his schedule to pick up the child and take her to her grandmother, who normally kept her on Wednesday nights because Natalie got home too late to disturb her parents and awaken their daughter for the trip home in the middle of the night.

Charlie can't remember what happened immediately after Natalie had spoken those sassy words. He remembers snatching her out of bed and putting his hands around her neck, but everything was a blur afterward until he snapped out of the trance he was in and realized somehow he must have snapped Natalie's neck, and now her body was limp. He was planning to get rid of Natalie, but not like this. He had planned to kill her in a way that her death would be seen as accidental. He was panicking, but he needed to calm down and think. It occurred to him that a fall downstairs was an accident wherein some victims did and some did not die from the fall. So he dragged Natalie from the bedroom, through the hallway, to the top of the stairs, and threw her down. She landed with her body in a supine position, arms splayed, and legs slightly apart with knees slightly bent. To any observer, it would appear that Natalie had tumbled backwards and fallen to her death.

Time was passing and Charlie needed to call and either postpone his appointment to later in the afternoon, or move it to another day. He made the call and was able to push the time up to 3 o'clock that afternoon. He left Natalie sprawled on the floor, locked the house, got in his car, and made it to the child day care center timely.

When Charlie took his little girl to her grandmother, he was harried and appeared impervious to conversation except to say that Natalie wasn't feeling well, again, and he was late for an appointment. Knowing that he was often distracted and rushing about, Mrs. Perkins took her grandchild inside so that Charlie could be on his way. He left hurriedly.

By this time, and after all that had transpired within a span of less than one and a half hours, Charlie's emotional bandwidth was stretched to its maximum capacity. But Charlie knew he had to keep thinking clearly if he hoped to get away with murder. So he doubled back home, locked himself inside, and tried to think. He knew he needed to report Natalie's death, but he was not yet calm enough to make the call. He needed a drink.

Charlie went to the bar and poured himself four fingers of Johnny Walker Red. He quickly gulped the Scotch down and chased it with a small glass of club soda. He swallowed some breath mints and now was beginning to relax a bit. He lifted the receiver of the home phone and dialed 911. When the emergency operator answered, Charlie told her he had just returned home and it appears that his wife has fallen down the stairs and was seriously injured. He asked the operator to send rescue personnel right away, and gave her the address. The operator asked Charlie if his wife was breathing, and he sated he didn't know. She instructed Charlie not to disturb anything, but to put his hand near her nose to see if she was breathing. Charlie complied and said he did not feel any air coming through her nostrils. The operator told Charlie that the rescue squad was on the way and would be there momentarily. She asked Charlie to see if he could feel his wife's pulse. By this time Charlie was moaning and pretending to be too upset to understand instructions offered by the emergency operator. He went out front and stood on the steps. As the ambulance was pulling into his driveway, Charlie was waving and beckoning it to come forward. Charlie proved to be a darn good actor because he had even managed to produce some tears by the time help had arrived.

It was obvious to the first responder examining Natalie that she was deceased. He immediately notified his team that they had a body that could not be moved until the coroner arrived and officially pronounced that Natalie had expired.

Zack Green had already been contacted about the situation and he was en route to the Pittman residence. When he arrived, one paramedic approached him as soon as he exited his vehicle and informed Zack that Charlie was acting suspiciously. He stated that Charlie had been pacing back and forth, interrupting them and asking too many questions, and asking repeatedly, "Is she dead?" after having been asked to refrain from interfering. At times he seemed confused and disoriented, and talked to himself incessantly. Zack thanked the paramedic for sharing his observation, but said it could all be because Charlie was in a state of shock. However, Charlie had had the presence of mind to call and cancel the 3 o'clock appointment.

Soon after Zack had arrived and entered the residence, he was informed that the coroner had been notified and would be arriving shortly. Some of Zack's deputies were securing the scene of the accident and potential crime with police tape in order to limit access and preserve contamination by curious neighbors who had begun to congregate in the Pittmans' yard.

"What has happened?" one neighbor asked no one in particular. Neighbors had seen Charlie standing outside before the first responders arrived, so they knew it had to be either Natalie or the child, Marcie, who might be hurt. As they were wondering and waiting, the coroner drove up. Someone in the group shouted, "Oh, my God! The coroner is here! Someone must be dead!"

Two more deputies arrived and asked the group of curious onlookers to move back farther away from the police tape, and the crowd complied, but not before another person asked the deputy what had happened inside the Pittman residence. The deputy did not make a response to the question.

Even though Charlie was acting as if he was suffering extreme emotional distress, and was not exhibiting his normal behavior, the sheriff noticed that Charlie had walked away from everyone and was talking on his home telephone. Charlie had called Mrs. Perkins to let her know that something had happened to Natalie. He did not want her to hear the news from anyone else first because he wanted his daughter to be kept away from drama and not be traumatized. Charlie had not even considered how upset Mrs. Perkins would be over news that her only child had been seriously injured from a fall. Charlie knew that Natalie was dead, but he did not say that to Mrs. Perkins. Charlie asked Mrs. Perkins to wait for further word on Natalie's condition before leaving home.

Mrs. Perkins was not going to stand by idly. How could she? How could that supercilious Charlie expect her to wait sangfroid while her child was hurt? She called her niece, Linda, who had just gotten off the afternoon school bus and asked her to come sit with little Marcie to allow her to go check on Natalie.

A pewter sky was losing the battle to brightness, and instead had begun to darken to a deeper shade of gray as Mrs. Perkins headed toward the Pittman home. A light drizzle began to fall, dampening the mood of the townspeople who, only six hours earlier, had awakened with expectations of going about a routine, monotonous, and uneventful day sanguine as opposed to a day of gloom that had permeated the atmosphere and settled over the town of Teaville, with the news of Natalie's death.

Natalie was a kind, sweet-spirited, loving girl, who was well liked by people who knew her, and she was the Perkinses' only beloved child. Until she married Charlie, she had never been known to abuse any substance. But lately her neighbors, members of her church, and general acquaintances had begun to wonder whether or not the marriage to Charlie, because of his aberrant behavior, had been the best thing for her, due to the drastic change she had made relative to her obvious abuse of some intoxicating substance, even though it became apparent later on that she was expecting at the time.. And there was still a tad of suspicion from some who knew Charlie that there was still what they presumed was a secret affair going on between him and Patricia Bailey. Natalie and Charlie only had one daughter. What a terrible blow this was to the Perkins family and their hope for the future! It placed a godforsaken blight on the Perkins family's future.

As Mrs. Perkins was turning into her daughter's driveway, the first thing she noticed was the coroner's minivan. She was walloped by an all-consuming grief, sending her spiraling downward, causing her to almost faint behind the wheel. She stopped on the spot, got out of her Chrysler Imperial and ran toward the house where she was caught by one of the deputies and told she could not enter the residence.

"But that's my daughter in there," she cried. "My baby! My baby! Oh, God, what has happened to my child?"

One of the neighbors who was still standing outside hoping to learn more about the situation placed a comforting arm around Mrs. Perkins' shoulder and held her gently against her chest. Mrs. Perkins was having a meltdown, and there was nothing that could be done except let her emotion run its course.

Inside, John Riverbank had pronounced Natalie dead, and was a bit distracted by all the commotion, without checking the body for any signs of foul play-- because it seemed obvious that she had taken a backward fall, and the death was accidental—and gave paramedics the OK to move the body. At the sight of her daughter being removed from her home in a body bag, Mrs. Perkins collapsed. Two of the first responders went to her and helped her get back into her vehicle. The neighbor who was offering comfort stayed with Mrs. Perkins as the first responders left with the other paramedics who had found Natalie and realized she was no longer alive.

Charlie had been slyly watching the movement and interaction. He ambled over to the Chrysler where Mrs. Perkins was sitting and continued his act of fake devastation. Mrs. Perkins was too distraught to notice or communicate with Charlie. She told the kindly neighbor that she needed to return home to be with her grandchild. She stated that she did not feel strong enough at the moment to drive herself, and asked to have someone drive her home. The kindly neighbor told

Mrs. Perkins that she would get her husband to follow them and she would take Mrs. Perkins home.

When all activity around the Pittman residence had subsided and Charlie was home alone with time to think clearly, he began pining for Patricia. He picked up the receiver and dialed her number. She answered after the first ring. The news had already reached her before she heard from Charlie. As she was expressing condolences to Charlie, he interrupted bluntly and said he needed to see her. Patricia said she didn't think that was a good idea for a while—she felt they needed to wait until at least after Natalie's funeral before they got together. And then it should be secretly because it would not be morally acceptable for them to be seen together so soon after his wife's death.

Charlie shouted, "To hell with that! I love you and I need you right now!"

Patricia asked Charlie to calm down and let her think. Then she asked Charlie if he could drive up to the university, leaving at 4 o'clock tomorrow morning, and she would sneak out of the dormitory and meet him at the main entrance promptly at 6 o'clock. Charlie said he would be there because he could hardly wait to hold her.

Throughout the night, all Charlie did was pace back and forth in the great room. He was too keyed up to sleep. He realized he had not seen little Marcie since everything had happened, but surmised it was no big deal because he wasn't that close to the child anyway. He would go see her after he had returned from his planned visit with Patricia.

At 3:30 Friday morning, Charlie left home and began the two-hour drive northwest. He reminded himself to be careful and not speed because he did not want his whereabouts known, so he did not need to be stopped and ticketed far away from home. Two hours later, Charlie parked at the main entrance to the university. He would have a 30-minute wait before Patricia arrived. And sure enough, promptly at 6 o'clock, there she was as she had promised.

Charlie got out and walked around the truck to open the door for her. But before he did, he grabbed her, squeezed her, and pressed her against his truck and devoured her lips with a deep passionate kiss. Both Charlie and Patricia were lost in the moment and pawing at one another as if this might be the last chance they would have to show their love for each other. Patricia caught her breath long enough to tell Charlie that they needed to get in the truck and leave. They were going to the motel where they always met to make love whenever Charlie would steal away to visit her at the university.

Once inside their motel room, they began stripping each other's clothes off as if they were in a race to some imaginary finish line. They mated their bodies together and fell onto the bed. He plowed deeper into her cavity and she pushed back matching every stroke. By the time they had landed on the mattress, they had climaxed together. It was the most magnificent self-fulfilling orgasm Patricia had ever experienced. They lay interlocked with one another in ecstasy for a long while. And then, with Charlie's maleness hardening again inside her, they began to oscillate together voraciously. She clasped her sex around him and squeezed love juices from his organ that brought them quickly to a heightened level of sexual satisfaction that neither of them had ever reached before. When he released his seed into her cavity, Patricia blissfully accepted every ounce of it, without regret. Neither of them was concerned about her getting pregnant at the moment because they knew now that they were free to get married, even though they knew they had to wait a while so that they would not shame themselves by behaving in a morally corrupt fashion. It was too soon to take any brazen actions.

After making love one more time, Patricia told Charlie he needed to return home because friends and neighbors would be looking for him to offer their condolences. It was now 8 o'clock. If he left within the next few minutes, he could be back home by 10 o'clock. As difficult as it was for them to separate at this time, Charlie dropped Patricia back at the main entrance to the university, and he headed back home.

Charlie dreaded the fate that would encompass him at home over the next few weeks and months. He had to find a way to conceal the fact that Patricia and he were bound together by a yearning so strong they were loathe to remain apart any longer. He wanted to marry Patricia immediately. Why wait for what other people considered a respectable period of time following his wife's death? What the heck was a respectable period? Six months? A year? Longer? There was no way he was going to wait that long to be with Patricia openly every minute he could spare. He was going to have her now, consequences be damned!

Another immediate problem facing Charlie was his need to hide the fact that Natalie did not die from an accidental fall. How could he prevent that snoop, John Riverbank, from picking Natalie apart? He would love to have her cremated right away, but he was sure Mrs.

Perkins would have a conniption if he suggested that as a course of action. And he didn't need any undue attention added to the near circus atmosphere that was permeating the community since friends and neighbors, alike, learned of Natalie's death. For his own protection, he needed to lay low and play it cool. He supposed he could play the part of a grieving spouse for a few days. He would have to! His freedom now depended upon how well he played his cards.

Charlie was thinking he not only longed to be bedded with Patricia at every opportunity because sex was so explosively fulfilling between them, his greatest desire was to have access to the Bailey checkbook. He was fed up with being a storm-chaser and listening to people whining and exaggerating losses they suffered from storm damage, or fires, or accidents in general. He had struggled to present a successful and respectable appearance practically all of his life, and he was tired of it. He was ready to live on easy street. And he was also ready to fulfill his dream of spending his days politicking—paving his way to the state capitol.

Charlie's dream of becoming a state senator has little to do with a desire to serve the people. His ambition had to do more with hobnobbing with men of stature and importance than serving a bunch of thankless hicks who were always looking for an easy way out; always pushing to get something for nothing. Sure, he would let them smile in his face with open hands, and they could bet, Charlie Pittman would be reciprocating their acts to a greater degree than they could imagine. He was so looking forward to bleeding the pockets of those wealthy souls who gave so generously to their legislators. In a few years, he would be a wealthy man— maybe even a rich one. He was going to become one of the graft-takers and play the game as well or better than the best of those old geezers who had been sitting on their duffs for years faking concern, falsely battling on behalf of constituents, and colluding with the opposite party in order to extend the hours of their false labor; and fooling big corporations into believing they were working for the benefit of their companies as hard as they could. What a joke! P.T. Barnum captured it best when he said, "There's a sucker born every minute."

As Charlie was approaching the outskirts of Teaville, he began to conjure up his game face. He had to play his part well for the sympathizers who would be dropping by to offer condolences. He will be so glad when this charade was over!

Back at the station, the sheriff was pondering points one of his deputies had brought to his attention about the way Charlie Pittman was acting at the scene of his wife's alleged accident. The sheriff was wondering if he should call the coroner and request a closer look at the body to determine if there was another cause of death other than an accidental fall. There was no need to rush and make a rash decision based on what appeared to have happened. Zack relied heavily on his deputies' good judgment and common sense; and in this case, there has been a continuous niggling in his conscience to be a bit more circumspect. It was common knowledge that Charlie was a cheater and an adulterer. So there was a possibility that Charlie crossed the line between decency and treachery.

As for Zack Green, Charlie had no respect for anyone who was as morally corrupt as the sheriff—especially when he was supposed to be setting an example of enforcing the law both morally and legally. Zack not only fathered a half-breed, he had operated a bootleg enterprise for as long as Charlie had known him. His partner in that crime was Clemis Stapleton. That was common knowledge. And who was naïve enough to think that Clemis left the area unbeknownst to Zack? Charlie knew better. As a matter of fact, to Charlie's way of thinking, Zack probably helped Clemis get away— perhaps he drove him some distance out of the county.

Who knows? Clemis' old pickup truck was still in his yard. Maybe time would tell. But in the meantime, the sheriff, if he had any suspicions about Natalie's death, had better ease up off of him, because Charlie was thinking he had dirt, if he used it correctly, that could bring the sheriff down. And Charlie was going to use every trick in the book to steer clear of a jail cell.

No one could say when, why, or how Charlie developed such a contemptuous attitude about men who accepted the responsibility of making favorable and necessary laws and statutes governing activities of daily living. Perhaps even Charlie himself didn't know. But Charlie sure proved, by his sinister thoughts and actions, that somewhere along the line he had somehow acquired an overdose of cynicism.

The sheriff had decided not to waste any more time debating the issue of whether or not he should make a request to the coroner asking him to conduct an autopsy on Natalie's body. So, he made the call. He shared his deputy's observation of Charlie's behavior with John Riverbank, and asked John to look for signs that the cause of death could have been by some other means rather than accidental. The coroner agreed and told the sheriff it was fine for him to proceed with notifying Charlie of his intent. Zack said he would personally deliver the news to Charlie so that he could check Charlie's reaction firsthand.

The sheriff contacted the deputy who had observed Charlie's unusual behavior after losing his wife, and asked him to accompany the sheriff to Charlie's home and to pay careful attention, once more, to Charlie's reaction when he learns that an autopsy would be performed on Natalie. In less than 30 minutes, they were on their way to deliver the news.

When Zack Green and his deputy arrived at the Pittman residence, the backyard and circular driveway were packed with cars. It seemed that everybody and his brother had come to offer condolences and pay respects to the Pittman and Perkins families. After they had parked and waded through a crowd in the backyard, Zack and his deputy entered the residence through a side door that opened into the Pittmans' great room. They spotted Charlie in a corner speaking with some members of the Presbyterian church they attended. When Charlie noticed the sheriff, he excused himself and came over to greet Zack. Charlie did not acknowledge the deputy. Charlie assumed Zack was just stopping by this time to offer condolences, and Charlie thanked Zack for being there. That's when Zack asked to speak with Charlie privately for just a moment. So, Charlie, Zack, with his deputy in tow, stepped into the kitchen. Zack then told Charlie that it was necessary to conduct an autopsy on Natalie in order to determine the exact cause of her death.

The color drained from Charlie's face and he stood there dumbfounded for a few seconds. Then he said, "She died from a fall, didn't she? Isn't that obvious?" But Zack told Charlie that Natalie could have died from a heart attack, or stroke, or some other cause first, and then could have fallen down the stairs after she was already dead. He said the cause of death must be accurate on the death certificate. Charlie said he did not want his wife all cut up. Zack made no response to that statement. Charlie's demeanor changed instantly from smiling and welcoming to cold and uninviting. His face began to twitch, his pupils pinpointed, his hands shook, he began to sweat, and his breathing became more rapid. Guests in the room had no indication that the sheriff was there on official business, and did not notice the metamorphosis in Charlie's mannerism and appearance.

After delivering the news, the sheriff and deputy headed back to the department. Charlie excused himself from his guests for a few minutes and ran upstairs to find Natalie's bottle of Prozac. He took two of the pills, then went to the bathroom and splashed cold water over his face. Leaning over the basin, he looked in the mirror and was floored by his haggard appearance. Then he thought, "This is good. As the grieving spouse, I'm supposed to look terrible." He dried his face and returned downstairs to his guests.

During the drive back to the department, Zack and his deputy discussed their observations of Charlie. Both men agreed that Charlie's behavior mimicked the actions of a guilty man. They had noticed his tremors, his sweating, the twitch, and the rapid breathing. They were convinced, albeit it circumstantial at this juncture, that Charlie was responsible for his wife's death. The sheriff left a message at the coroner's office to have the coroner call him as soon as possible.

The next day, after she had time to calm herself and think clearly, Olivia Perkins wondered if Charlie was capable of planning her daughter's funeral. She had already taken the time to try and explain to Little Marcie that her mother was now living in Heaven with God, and what it was like in Heaven. Marcie was really too young to grasp the concept, but she told her grandmother that if she could no longer have her mother, she wanted to live with Mrs. Perkins. Olivia felt there could be no greater gift than having her granddaughter living with her all the time. It would help fill the void in her life that has been left from losing her only daughter. She would ask Charlie if this could be arranged. With him on the go all the time, perhaps he would agree. She would go to him and offer her help in planning the funeral, and she would use that opportunity to ask about keeping Little Marcie.

Later in the afternoon, Mrs. Perkins asked Linda to look after Little Marcie again while she went to see Charlie. It was a beautiful sunny day. A warm breeze was blowing, and Mrs. Perkins found Charlie sitting out back on the deck when she arrived. He was sipping what appeared to be lemonade, and he offered Olivia lemonade or iced tea. She declined a drink. She asked Charlie if he was doing OK and stated she had come to speak to him about making funeral arrangements. Charlie told Olivia that the pathologist was performing an autopsy on Natalie's body and it would be several days before the body would be released. He said that they should arrange a private service for the family only on Friday morning at 11 o'clock, followed by a brief graveside service at noon. He said that way it would be convenient for anyone who needed to use the lunch hour to attend the service. Mrs. Perkins agreed and asked Charlie if he would like her to call Orion-McDowell

Funeral Home to make the arrangements. Charlie nodded in the affirmative and thanked Olivia for her help. In Olivia's opinion, Charlie appeared to be nervous and anxious for her to leave, so she did not linger.

Friday was a gloomy day. There was a light drizzle in the early morning that had upgraded to a downpour by 11 o'clock. The church service was short and as the funeral cortege was approaching the cemetery, there was a sea of black umbrellas where friends and neighbors were standing in heavy rain, oblivious to the unfavorable weather conditions. The graveside service was over in 20 minutes, then the majority of attendees dashed to their vehicles and drove a half mile to the Teaville Community Center where repast was being served.

Once everyone had gathered inside the building, the noise was deafening. Old friends were chatting; there was yelling across the room to gain attention, all against the backdrop of sounds from the clanging and clatter of serving utensils and noise from the kitchen. The mood was not somber. On the contrary, the atmosphere was exuberant. Mr. and Mrs. Perkins were pleased to see so many well-wishers and sympathizers. It beamed all over their faces. But on the other hand, Charlie seemed depressed. He was communicating minimally with friends and neighbors who offered condolences. He kept watching the entrance as if he were expecting someone. Even though Patricia had told him she would not make an appearance at his wife's funeral, Charlie kept hoping she would change her mind and be there for him. He felt strongly that he needed her, and he didn't care what people thought about them being together so soon after Natalie's death.

The week following Natalie's funeral, the Grand Jury met in the town of Marigold. Zack Green, his deputy, and John Riverbank testified before the jurors and presented evidence relating to Natalie's alleged accident and subsequent death. The coroner presented evidence that indicated Natalie had died from a broken neck, but the break did not happen as a result of the fall down the stairs. He stated that the bruising on the body was inconsistent with a backward tumble down the stairs. The coroner said it was his professional opinion that Natalie had been thrown from the second floor of her home, and he used diagrams to illustrate and support his conclusion. The coroner said he had conferred with some of his colleagues who are acclaimed as the best in the field of forensic pathology, and they concurred with his findings.

When the sheriff testified, he told the jurors that he and his number one deputy interviewed Charlie Pittman on the day of his wife's death and the day after. He shared their observations and stated that Charlie had presented all the signs of a guilty person. He cited Charlie's tremors, sweating, twitching, and breathing— all signs that any professional psychologist or psychiatrist would acknowledge as symptoms of guilt. And when the deputy testified, he corroborated everything the sheriff had presented in his testimony. Time would tell whether Charlie would be indicted or not.

A few days later, word was spreading through Teaville and other towns in Kinder County that Charlie Pittman, the onetime sports figure, and current insurance adjuster, had been indicted on charges of murdering his wife. While some folks found it hard to fathom, others believed Charlie was capable of committing the crime. And for those who believed it, news of Charlie's arrest brought enormous relief. David and Olivia Perkins were shocked beyond measure. Mr. Perkins became physically ill and had to be rushed to the hospital for emergency nerve-calming treatment. After several hours under observation at the hospital, he was allowed to return home.

When Joe Bailey and Patricia received news of Charlie's arrest, Joe wasn't in much better shape than David Perkins had been when the news reached him. Patricia actually fainted when she learned what had happened to Charlie. Joe was as angry as he had ever been in his life that the pariah, Charlie Pittman, had tainted his daughter with his smooth talking and cunning character. And Patricia, in her innocence, was planning to marry this creep. Joe said it would only happen over his dead body. He could hardly wait for Charlie to be tried, convicted, and sent to prison. Hopefully, they would send Charlie to a prison west of Hell, and that wouldn't be far enough away from Teaville as far as Joe was concerned.

After Patricia had slept for six hours, she woke up determined to stick by Charlie. She did not believe he was capable of killing anyone—least of all Natalie. How dare they arrest Charlie! She needed her daddy to calm down and start pulling some strings to get Charlie out of this mess. Her daddy's motto was "Money Talks!" So now she needed his money to talk to the right people who could award Charlie his freedom. She would wait until tomorrow morning to speak to her daddy.

The following morning bright and early, Joe was in the kitchen enjoying his morning cup of coffee. He was waiting for Patricia to come downstairs so they could discuss the dissolution of her relationship with Charlie Pittman once and for all. A few minutes later, he heard her footsteps as she was making her way to the kitchen.

"Morning, Daddy," she said in her usual cheerful manner. And she kissed the bald spot in the top of his head.

"Hello, honey," Joe replied. "I was waiting for you to come downstairs so we can talk."

Patricia said, "I want to talk to you too, Daddy. I need you to help me get Charlie released from jail."

Patricia was about to say something further, but Joe interrupted her so suddenly that she was taken aback.

Joe said, "I'll be damned if I'll do anything of the sort! He's nothing but a piece of trash, and I forbid you to continue a relationship with him!"

"But Daddy, Charlie and I are going to be married!"

"Like Hell you are!"

Patricia burst out crying and ran back upstairs, slammed and locked the door to her room.

She could be heard crying out loud behind the closed door.

Suddenly, Joe felt he needed some brandy in his coffee, and he poured a bit into his cup. He loved Patricia and he had always let her have her way. Now, after all these years, he was sorry he had spoiled her. But he was not going to let her ruin her life because of a no-good scoundrel. He simply could not allow it! When Patricia calmed down, he would try and reason with her some more.

Patricia remained locked in her room, refusing to speak to her daddy. She would come downstairs when Joe left home to handle business matters, but when he returned, she would retreat to her room again. After four days of this drama, Joe relented, stood outside Patricia's bedroom, and told her he would see if there was anything he could do to help Charlie if she would stop acting childish and come out of her room and communicate like an adult. He went back downstairs.

It wasn't long before Patricia joined Joe in the great room. He was upset at the sight of her. It was plain to see that she had lost weight. She had dark circles under her red puffy eyes, and she was unkempt. Her hair had not been combed and she was wearing the same outfit she had been wearing when he saw her four days ago. Joe picked up the phone and called their family physician. When Dr. Dean came on the line, Joe told him he needed the doctor to make a house call as soon as possible. Dr. Dean said he could be there in an hour.

After Patricia had been examined and given a sedative, Joe and Dr. Dean had a long talk. Dr. Dean told Joe it would be better for him to play along with Patricia so she could snap out of the depression she was in. Joe said he would do anything for his daughter. He said he would post the $1.5 million bond to get Charlie released from jail, and he would see what happened after that.

When Joe told Patricia he was going to stand bond for Charlie, she snapped back to her old self so quickly, Joe wondered if he had been conned by his daughter. Nevertheless, he was relieved to see a semblance of Patricia's old self inhabiting her body.

When word spread through communities that Joe Bailey had posted bond for Charlie Pittman, many people were not surprised, but some folks were shocked. Among those most shocked were David and Olivia Perkins. They were so upset over the fact that Charlie was the cause of their daughter's death, they were hoping he would rot in jail—even if he is their only grandchild's father. Because Joe had buckled under pressure from his daughter, some of his friends began to distance themselves from him.

People were demanding swift justice for Natalie when they learned Charlie had been released from jail. Since this was an election year, the responsible officials who were running for re-election scheduled Charlie's trial to begin in 90 days. Charlie's attorney did not object because he felt that the only evidence against Charlie was circumstantial. He felt that winning this case would be a piece of cake. And as it turned out, he was right. When his trial was held, Charlie was acquitted. The Perkinses were devastated. Joe Bailey's money had spoken loud and clear.

PART V

Since the time she was 3 years old, Little Lizzie hated her Uncle Sammy. He always dominated her mother's time. Although Janie, her mother, was the only living sibling of Sammy's, in Little Lizzie's mind that didn't give him the right to drop by anytime he had a notion to, because by doing so, he disrupted the peaceful, loving atmosphere that Little Lizzie and her mother often enjoyed. It was their bonding time. And after all, he lived next door, so he could not claim to have missed seeing them. He saw them every day. He never knocked when he came over.

Sammy would walk in freely, because the door was never locked, and demand that Janie stop whatever she was doing and, more often than not, prepare a meal for him. To look at him, he could have missed more than a few meals. Only 5 foot, 8 inches tall, he weighed more than 250 pounds. He seemed to always want a spread of food that had to be cooked on the spot. His favorite was fried chicken, macaroni and cheese, cabbage, and hot biscuits. So, invariably, Janie would scurry about the kitchen to meet Sammy's immediate demand. Feeling ignored by her mother, and seeing her dancing to her Uncle Sammy's music, angered Little Lizzie immeasurably for a little prissy girl. Over time, Little

Lizzie vowed that she would one day find a way to punish Uncle Sammy for his rude and inconsiderate ways.

Eventually, Little Lizzie began to resent Janie for catering to Sammy's every whim, because in essence, Janie was giving time and attention to Sammy, which in Little Lizzie's mind, should have been given to her.

As the years passed, Lizzie was no longer Little Lizzie, but grew up to become a vibrant teen who morphed into an energetic, resourceful young woman. It would be a stretch to describe Lizzie as beautiful, but one could say she was a nice-looking young girl. She had a brilliant mind, although she never used it to its full potential according to many of her teachers. She had big, beautiful brown eyes that could be piercing when Lizzie was angered by anyone or anything. She could be considered tall for a girl—she was 5 foot, 9 inches tall. And she was blessed with velvety bronze skin. Although her dark auburn hair was kinky, it was long and thick, making her the envy of many other young girls who weren't so amply endowed.

Immediately following high school graduation, Lizzie chose not to attend college because she wanted to earn an income for herself, mostly because she was anxious to get away from her worrisome uncle. During her lifetime, Lizzie had thoughts of Janie and Sammy as two people in a bottomless pit. She felt this way because neither her mother nor her uncle had a 9-to-5, five-day-per-week job like most other adult neighbors in the community. Many of their neighbors were progressive, professional, and more middle class than Janie and Sammy. Janie had survived through the years on the survivor's annuity she received for herself and Lizzie following the death of her husband, Lizzie's father. And Sammy received a small disability check due to an injury he had received following an accident years ago. Neither Janie nor Sammy owned a vehicle. They had to depend on distant relatives or neighbors for transportation. Because in rural Kinder County where they resided, there was no public transportation.

Another one of Lizzie's dreams was, in addition to earning an income, she had a great desire to own a car. That way she could do the grocery shopping for herself and her mom any time she felt the need, and would not have to wait until it was convenient for someone else to take them shopping at a ridiculous charge. She would also be able to transport her mom to her medical appointments in a timely fashion.

Both Janie and Sammy used the excuse that they received survivor's and disability benefits as the primary reason neither of them had a job. But in Lizzie's opinion, that was a disgusting way to live. It was a distasteful thought for Lizzie because she always believed that both her mother and uncle were capable of engaging in gainful employment as well.

Over time, Kinder County powerbrokers began to entice more industries to the area. That brought jobs that would enable many of the county's citizens to work in their home county rather than have to commute to surrounding counties to find near living-wage jobs. Lizzie was fortunate to be among those hired at the boat company located in Kinder County, which was a distance of 16 miles from her home. Shooter Boat Company was located on a tributary of the Northeast Cape Dread River, and offered an ideal site for shipwrights.

Lizzie vowed to be one of the best employees Shooter Boat Company employed. And as her supervisor would later attest, Lizzie was one of the best employees at the company. At her six-month evaluation, Lizzie was granted a promotion that added a $2-per-hour increase to her salary. She was elated. Lizzie decided at that point, she was in a position to purchase a compact vehicle that gave very good gas mileage because she had to cover 32 miles round-trip from her home to the boat factory and back, five days per week. By this time, she was no longer entertaining the notion of leaving home as soon as she could find a suitable place to live. She would be stuck in Hilliston for a while.

The very first Saturday Lizzie went car shopping, she was fortuitous enough to stop at a dealership where the famous Johnny B. Goode was the top car salesman. Johnny was always on the lookout for a new potential customer, and he spotted Lizzie the moment she hopped out of her friend's old Ford Falcon. In his usual fashion, he approached Lizzie with professional courtesy and a smile that could melt a girl's heart. Lizzie immediately felt special and that this was going to be her lucky day. She explained her situation to Mr. Goode, including the need for a vehicle that was conservative on gasoline, and that she had only saved a minimal amount for a down payment. She wanted a nice compact car, but could not afford a brand new vehicle. Johnny, being a master at memorizing inventory, felt he had just the right vehicle for Lizzie to consider. The vehicle he showed her was a 1960 four-door Corvair. Lizzie could hardly contain her excitement. Having four doors, the car would be perfect for transporting her mom, groceries, and other items they might purchase during a shopping trip.

Lizzie liked the car on the spot and asked Mr. Goode if they could take it for a test drive. He said, "Sure, but call me Johnny." So, he dashed into the showroom, went to his office to sign out, and returned with the keys to the 1960, four-door, navy blue Corvair. Lizzie felt a tickling sensation all over her body as she got behind the wheel. They drove for a few miles as Johnny pointed out specifics about the car. When they returned to the car lot, before Johnny could speak, Lizzie asked to go to his office to discuss terms for purchasing the Corvair.

Since Lizzie still lived at home with her mother, during the six-month period that she had been working at Shooter Boat Company, she had been able to save $1,200. When Johnny had completed the paperwork, Lizzie had enough for a $600 down payment and funds to cover tags, title, and taxes. From now on, she would not have to depend on anyone to carpool to her job. But she knew she would not be able to continue saving $200 per month because she would have to cover gasoline purchases and pay for vehicle insurance and maintenance.

Needless to say, the purchase of her vehicle posed a new set of problems that Lizzie had not considered. The primary problem being Uncle Sammy. In his usual selfish fashion, he expected Lizzie to taxi him wherever he wanted to go when her workday ended. He did not care, and it did not matter how exhausted she was. He also expected to be driven wherever his heart led him on Saturdays and Sundays. This would leave little, or no, time for Lizzie to manage her personal affairs and complete errands for Janie. Being the passive sister that she was, Janie always encouraged Lizzie to take Uncle Sammy hither and yonder. Lizzie was becoming more and more furious, both at her mom and her uncle.

Lizzie was beginning to have nightmares about her mom and uncle pestering her. She began to confide in her closest friend at the boat factory that she was sick and tired of her mother and uncle treating her as their slave. Some days during their lunch break, Lizzie would be so angry over some demand they had made on the previous evening that she could not eat lunch. She began to say that she wanted to be rid of those two people. Her friend Alma suggested that she move and get a place to rent that would be closer to her job and farther away from her mom and uncle. But Lizzie stated that she could not afford an apartment because she did not earn enough money to cover a car note plus rent. She was living in her mom's house free-of-charge. But seeing Lizzie's tirades, Alma began to worry about Lizzie's mental health and well-being. Alma was beginning to have foreboding thoughts.

Lizzie felt that she was caught in a whirlwind and she was spinning out of control. She felt helpless because in her mind's eye there was nowhere to turn for relief. So, Lizzie began to have sinister thoughts about her situation and what she could do to bring about a transformation. She knew that she could not afford to move. And why should she? It was her home as much as it was her mother's. When her daddy died, he had willed the home to Lizzie and her mother. So Lizzie decided she wasn't leaving. Continuing to live there could be bearable if it weren't for the fact that Uncle Sammy lived next door. "No!" Lizzie thought. "There has to be another way!" So, Lizzie devised a plan.

It was noonday one Saturday not long after Lizzie had been having thoughts that would enable her to gain freedom from the bondage she felt relative to Uncle Sammy—then he, the Devil himself, came sauntering through the front door demanding to know what they were having for lunch. Lizzie cringed when Janie said that they had not yet prepared lunch, but she would gladly fix something for him. To which Sammy bellowed, "Since you have to fix it, fry me some chicken. I can wait." It was this sort of cockiness that made Lizzie's blood boil.

Even though Lizzie had planned to wait several weeks before putting her thoughts into action because she wanted her plan to be fail-safe, she made a sudden decision on the spot that fate had delivered her the opportunity on this very day. She was not going to wait any longer. She decided at that very moment that she was going to take care of the situation the next day. She was going to prepare a meal for Uncle Sammy that he would never forget.

When the sun rose the next day, Lizzie was restless and overloaded with anxiety. She was anxious to begin preparing their Sunday meal. Following breakfast, she quickly cleaned the kitchen and told Janie that she would prepare Sunday lunch, and Janie did not have to worry about it. Janie was delighted. She could not remember a time over the last five years that Lizzie had volunteered to cook. As a matter of fact, to Janie's recollection, in all the years since she had taught Lizzie how to prepare meals, Lizzie had never volunteered for kitchen duty of any kind.

A few months earlier, Janie and Lizzie had been bothered with mice, and Janie had purchased some bags of a strong rat killer and some liquid d-CON to get rid of them. The unused poison was stored in the shed out back. When Janie lay down for a nap at 10:30 that morning as was part of her Sunday routine on the Sundays they did not have church service, Lizzie took a large bowl to the shed and filled it with the powder. She returned to the kitchen and began to make a batter of cornbread. She knew that Janie did not like cornbread, but Sammy loved it. She added some cracklings to better camouflage the taste of the poison she poured into the meal batter. She also used more sugar than she ordinarily used to ensure the flavor tasted the way Sammy liked it. He loved to have a bit of sugar added to all of the breads Janie prepared for him, and Lizzie remembered that. Lizzie made a gallon of iced tea that she loaded with the strong liquid poison. She added lots of sugar and plenty of sliced lemons to obscure any taste of the poison. She even added honey to the mixture to further conceal the taste of the poison.

After Lizzie had doused the meal batter with poison, added cracklings and sugar, she set it aside. She did not want to put the cornbread in the oven too soon because she wanted it to be hot, just the way Sammy liked it. Next, Lizzie put on a pot of green beans, and when she had completed that task, she began to peel Irish potatoes. She was going to make creamed mashed potatoes—another of Sammy's favorite dishes. She put the potatoes on to boil and set the skillet on the burner to have it ready for frying chicken. She sprinkled paprika over all the chicken and then coated each piece with flour. Before turning on the burner under the skillet, she went next door to inform Sammy that she would be bringing over lunch for him at noon. Sammy was tickled over the fact that he was going to get another free lunch from Janie and Lizzie. After Lizzie left, he kicked back in his recliner and dozed into a stage three sleep.

Next door, Lizzie removed the boiled potatoes from the pot and put them in a dish where she would mash them and add cream. When she felt they were fluffy enough, she added a little poison and a dash of sugar to them as well. She used a separate bowl to mashed potatoes for Janie and herself. She knew Janie only liked butter on her mashed potatoes and she definitely did not like them sweet.

At 11:30 a.m. the green beans had cooked and were ready to be served. Lizzie had the oven heated to just the right temperature for Sammy's pan of cornbread, and the pan of biscuits she had made for Janie. She placed the pans in the oven. A few minutes later, Janie woke up to the smell of chicken frying and bread baking. She realized that she had an appetite for lunch. She got up, went into the kitchen, complimented Lizzie on how good everything smelled, and thanked her for the kindly deed she had done. Lizzie assured Janie that it was a pleasure and everything would be ready at 12 o'clock.

At 11:50 a.m., Lizzie dished up some green beans to drain; she filled a bowl with creamed potatoes, took the hot bread from the oven, and placed Sammy's favorite parts of the chicken on a plate. She added green beans to the plate; wrapped the cornbread in aluminum foil, and covered the potatoes with foil; and put everything in a shopping bag and told Janie she was taking lunch to Sammy and would return immediately to have lunch with her.

Sammy was mighty pleased when Lizzie walked through his door bringing lunch. He bolted up from the recliner and went straight to the table, where Lizzie placed the food she had prepared. Lizzie told Sammy she had to return home and have lunch with Janie. Sammy understood and really wasn't interested in anything Lizzie had to say, as he had already begun eating his meal. He didn't even bother to thank Lizzie, which was typical of him.

Lizzie and Janie were chatting merrily and enjoying a meal together without a disruption from Sammy when suddenly Janie said, "As soon as we finish our meal, I think I will go next door for a visit with

Sammy for a while this afternoon." Lizzie told Janie that she would clean up after them so she could visit her brother as long as she liked. When Janie left to go next door, Lizzie put the leftovers away, cleaned the kitchen, and took a nap. Lizzie had not realized how strenuous it was to prepare a meal since she was not accustomed to doing so. She fell into an exhaustive sleep and did not wake up until 6 o'clock in the evening. Lizzie realized immediately that Janie had not yet returned from her visit with Sammy.

Earlier in the afternoon, around 3 o'clock, Sammy had told Janie that he was hungry again. Actually, he was greedy because he knew there was food left over from lunch. So he and Janie went back into the kitchen and dished up the leftovers. Although Janie did not like sweetened creamed mashed potatoes, she decided she would eat some just this once, since Lizzie had sent over a big bowl full that was really too much for Sammy to finish in one day. While she was at it, she said she might as well eat some cornbread, too, since Lizzie had cooked a large pan full and sent it all to Sammy. So, she and Sammy ate again, finishing the gallon of iced tea, and gossiped about the happenings in Kinder County. Among the back chat they had heard were plenty of rumors about old rich Hugh Manson over in Anderson and how the talk was that he might have had sweet Mrs. Elizabeth burned up, or had done it himself. Everyone was paused to see how that catastrophe would play out.

While they were gabbing, both of them began to feel woozy. So, they left the table and flopped back down in the recliners. Soon, both Sammy and Janie were sleeping soundly. And while they were sleeping, their breathing became shallow; their heartbeats slowed; and within several hours they both were deceased.

***

It was getting close to 7 in the evening and Janie still had not returned. Lizzie decided to go next door to see if Janie was still visiting with Sammy, or whether she had decided to visit their neighbor Miss Trudy who lived two houses a short distance down the road.

Lizzie, as usual, did not knock before entering through the back door of Sammy's home. She didn't hear the sound of voices as she walked towards the parlor—only the sound of a jingle coming from the television. Sammy and Janie must have fallen asleep. When Lizzie approached her mother, she was about to shake her, but noticed that Janie's head was tilted at an odd angle. Then she noticed foam sliding out of one corner of Janie's mouth. She turned and looked at

Sammy and his pose nearly mirrored the slant of Janie's. Lizzie's heart began pounding rapidly and so strong that she could hear as well as feel the pulsation pounding through her body. She began to sweat profusely and her hands were shaking as she turned back to Janie to feel her pulse. Janie had no pulse.

It suddenly occurred to Lizzie that Janie must have eaten some of the food she had fixed for Sammy's craw only. "Oh, God!" she mumbled to no one in particular. "What have I done?" Lizzie was shocked over the act she realized she was guilty of, but not so shocked that she wasn't thinking that she needed to act with break-neck speed to cover this mistake. It was an accident she was telling herself. Yes, it was an unfortunate accident on Janie's part for eating Sammy's food, but Lizzie, even though she knew she had deliberately schemed to get rid of Sammy, was denying any responsibility for Janie's death. So, what was she going to do now? She had just murdered two people—one of whom was her mother.

Lizzie got busy cleaning up and trying to cover up the mess she had made. First, she took all of the food—bowls and containers included—and threw everything in a large garbage bag. Then she wet a towel and cleaned Janie's face and Sammy's face. She repositioned their heads so it would appear that they had simply kicked back in the recliners and fallen asleep. She looked around carefully to be sure she had cleared any signs of evidence that could create any suspicion that a crime had taken place. When she was satisfied that the surroundings were staged to look natural, she went next door and drove her car over to Sammy's house, parking it at the back door that opened into the kitchen. She looked all around to be sure there were no passersby who could later give an account of what she was doing. When she felt the coast was clear, she put the garbage in her Corvair. She went back into the house, looked around one more time, then from the kitchen she stepped onto the back porch, closed the door, got into her vehicle, and drove one mile to the Dumpster. She looked around and made sure she was alone at the dump site, and then she exited her Corvair and threw the garbage bag into the trash bin.

On the drive back home Lizzie remembered all the poison that was out back in the shed. She parked at the shed, opened her trunk, and began nervously placing all the poison into the open compartment. Abruptly, all of a sudden, she did not want the poison to spill in her car so she ran inside and snatched two trash bags from the pantry. She went back outside and began frantically placing the poison in the trash bags. When she had finished, she drove back to the dump site, and repeated the ritual she had performed only a few minutes earlier.

When Lizzie had completed her acts to cover up the crime she had committed, she sat down at her mother's kitchen table and tried to think. It was getting late and she knew she needed to call and report that she had found her mother and uncle asleep and she could not wake them. She knew she would have to answer a whole lot of senseless questions and not get caught in a lie. And she also knew that if she played her cards right, the sheriff or whoever came to the scene, would call the coroner who would declare that two people were dead. And she was hoping that not much attention would be given to the cause of death, and their deaths would be written off as congestive heart failure because the victims were elderly and Black; and as far as the rest of the world was concerned, they were two more no-account souls bound for Heaven or Hell. No big deal. So, Lizzie composed herself and prepared to make the call.

People who thought they knew Lizzie were unaware that she had a mean streak because Lizzie hid behind a bright smile. She could be cold and calculating when she wasn't having her way. She had been that way ever since she was a very young girl. At 4 years old she liked to play outside and kill anything that was alive, moving, and within her reach. She started out killing bugs and butterflies, and gradually as she grew older, killed frogs, varmints, and larger animals. When cats would disappear from the neighborhood, the assumption was that they had moved on to a different home or taken to the wild. But in actuality, most of the time the disappearance was a result of Little Lizzie's handiwork. She used her daddy's crowbar that had supposedly been discarded when he no longer moonlighted part time as a carpenter.

As Lizzie grew older, when things didn't go her way, she would have ghastly thoughts—often about killing whoever was the object of her ire. So, at an early age, when she began to contemplate that she would one day get rid of Uncle Sammy, the idea was deeply rooted into her psyche so she was destined to act on this desire at some time in the future.

Discovering that her mother had mistakenly been poisoned to death as a result of her greediness—because she could not have been hungry—did not upset Lizzie as any normal person would have been affected under such aberrant circumstances. Lizzie was not a normal person and killing was not abnormal in Lizzie's case; it was commonplace, the norm, and had been since childhood.

Having to cover up her sinister deed was not as emotionally and psychologically taxing for Lizzie as it would be for a stable individual. Lizzie was neurotic, and all of her life she had been able to cunningly conceal her true self. Lizzie was selfish, shrewd, hardened, and grossly perverse.

***

It had been a relatively quiet Sunday for the Emergency Operations Center, but at 9:30 Sunday night the 911 emergency operator took a call from a hysterical female who seemed so distraught she could hardly make herself understood. When the operator was finally able to get Lizzie to calm down a bit, she understood that two people needed help. It was the caller's mother and uncle, if the operator was understanding correctly. They were located in Hilliston Township. The address was 504-B Hilliston Road. Once the operator had dispatched the information to first responders and they were en route to the address, the operator began to ask the caller a second series of questions.

"What is your name?"

"Lizzie McPherson."

"What is your relationship to the two individuals?"

"It's my mother and my uncle."

"What is your mother's name?"

"Janie McPherson and my uncle is Sammy DeWitt."

"Can you tell me if they are breathing OK?"

"I don't know! I don't know!"

"Can you check for me? See if Miss Janie is breathing?"

No response.

"Hello, Lizzie? Are you still with me?"

No response.

The operator continued to try and get Lizzie to acknowledge that she was still on the line, but Lizzie refused to respond. Lizzie had turned the light on and was standing on the front porch when the paramedics arrived. When they approached her, she pointed inside.

Lizzie's response to all questions relative to what had happened here was, "I don't know." The only enlightenment she shared—which wasn't much—was, "This is the way I found them and I dialed 911 immediately because I could not wake them up."

As paramedics were examining the two victims, Lizzie sat catatonically staring straight ahead, looking at nothing in particular. When one of the other first responders attempted to question Lizzie about her mother's health in general, she realized that Lizzie had completely shut down. The female paramedic thought perhaps she might be able to break through the wall that Lizzie had built around her mind. Lizzie felt safe in the place she had ventured to mentally, and no smiley-faced woman was going to draw her out of it.

Realizing that Lizzie had zoned out, the female paramedic asked Lizzie if there was anyone she could call to come be with her during this unfortunate ordeal. Lizzie shook her head to indicate "no" and said, "I'll be OK."

By this time the coroner, who happened to have been passing through the area when he received the call, was pulling into Sammy's driveway. John Riverbank had been traveling back home from Mockston, where he had spent all day Sunday visiting several friends. He had been on the outskirts of Hilliston when the call came through, so he exited off Interstate 400 onto Highway 111, which placed him only a half mile from Hilliston Road.

It took John less than eight minutes to examine and pronounce both Sammy and Janie deceased. Hearing John's conclusion, Lizzie stepped forward and said she would like to call Munn's Funeral and Cremation Service to come pick up the bodies. When the coroner stated he would like to examine the two bodies further in order to determine the exact cause of death, Lizzie said both of them had had bad hearts, and she doesn't know what caused them to pass away when they did, but they must have had heart attacks. Perhaps something frightened them; or maybe something they saw on television scared them to death. John was exhausted from having been out of town the weekend and driving all day from Mockston, so he gave the OK for Munn to pick up the bodies and signed off on the cause of death as congestive heart failure. While outwardly Lizzie continued to present the appearance of being brokenhearted and disconsolate, deep down she was intoxicated with a sense of victory and relief over how she had duped the coroner. Partly because her prediction had proven to be true that the death of the two elderly people would be insignificant and listed as congestive heart failure, and partly because John Riverbank was too tired to probe deeper for some other clue that would shed a different light on the cause of those two deaths.

The funerals of Janie and Sammy were held without the usual fanfare that customarily happens when popular, middle-class members of the Hilliston community pass away. Janie and Sammy had led quiet ordinary lives and, for the most part, had distanced themselves from their middle-class neighbors. But some of the neighbors did show their respects primarily because they were feeling sorry for Lizzie, who was now left alone in the world. But country folks can be counted on to pitch in and help when a neighbor is in need. So, in all likelihood, Lizzie was going to be alright. She had a home, a job, and a vehicle.

Two days after the funeral, Lizzie returned to work looking revitalized and happy. Her demeanor gave no indication that she was grieving the loss of her mother and uncle. When she sat down during lunch with her friend Alma, she ate ravenously and chatted with Alma and said nothing in her life had changed, except for the fact that she had gotten rid of two pests. Alma was afraid to ask Lizzie what she meant, so she pretended not to hear Lizzie's response and politely changed the subject. Alma thought to herself that her friend Lizzie must have a split personality, and she made a mental note to always keep the climate between herself and Lizzie warm and sunny. Alma knew that at this juncture, there was no point in ever mentioning what Lizzie had said. It would be her secret.

EPILOGUE

Nearly five years have passed. Peggy and Casper have experienced the rite of passage into the world where teenagers purport to have lost all childhood tendencies. They believe they have crossed the Rubicon into young adulthood.

Peggy and Casper are making plans for life after high school, already focusing on their courses of study for accomplishing their life-long professions, and hoping to maintain the 4.5 grade point averages they have earned as a result of having high aptitudes and excellent study habits. Although they are only in grade 11 with another year and a half before high school graduation, both of them have set their sights on their university of choice.

Peggy likens Harvard to the next step before Heaven, and will receive the disappointment of her young lifetime if her application is declined when she is in a position to apply. Over the years she has listened to adults speak with respect and admiration of John Riverbank with his keen acumen for solving murder mysteries, which otherwise would have been set aside for the wrong reasons, due to a lack of knowledge and skills in pathology and forensics. Were it not for John's insight and problem-solving abilities, the outcome of many cases would be totally different. He is the primary reason Peggy has decided she would like to study forensic pathology.

Peggy admires John Riverbank's unwavering tenacity to delve into the nuts and bolts of what would appear to be unsolvable problems and never giving up until he gets to the bottom of the exact cause of death—even with bodies that some of his colleagues consider burned beyond the capacity of making an accurate analysis and finding.

Whereas a few years ago Peggy and Casper were planning to get as far away as possible from Kinder County and their homes in the Hawk Town community, Peggy now wants to follow in John Riverbank's footsteps. She hopes to get an excellent education and then return home to work as John's assistant, if he will have her after she passes the necessary Xenolina State exams. Maybe one day when John retires, she might become the pathologist appointed to the position he vacates. She realizes it's a long shot, but Peggy has never in her young lifetime shied away from a challenge.

As for Casper, he has dreams of his own. However, his dreams do not include attending an Ivy League university so far away from home. He will be content if he is accepted at an in-state university to complete a four-year degree in criminal justice. While he has never shared his deepest dream with anyone—not even Peggy—and he never intends to, he believes what he has in mind is achievable, and he is working toward that end.

***

On the first day of August nearly five years ago, Joyce gave birth to a beautiful 8 pound, 9 ounce, healthy baby boy. The birth of their son completed Joyce and Teddy's world. They named their son Victor, and he is loved and cared for by everyone in the Jones and Stapleton families.

Victor is a very active handsome 4½-year-old ham. He is often seen in the fields chasing crickets or rabbits or anything movable while Teddy, although tending crops, is keeping a watchful eye on his son. When Victor is at home with Joyce or the girls, he is usually on the floor coloring, reading, or playing with toys. He shows signs of being an unusually bright child, and Joyce intends to keep him engaged in learning activities. Her co-workers at school continue to provide books and materials that challenge Victor's developing brain.

When Teddy settles down after dinner tonight, Joyce has a bit of news to share with him. In seven months, Victor is going to have a brother or sister.

***

After having worked tirelessly for nearly five years, Dancie has been contemplating taking a vacation in the foreseeable future. She is now in a position to take time and unwind because as her business outgrew her ability to manage every detail alone, she hired two local young ladies to assist with cooking and serving sandwiches and meals. She also hired an accountant who manages receipts on a part-time basis. Additionally, Dancie has equipped her business with neon flashing lights that advertise and invite all who love to dance and enjoy fine dining to come spend some time at Dancie's Place. It promises to be an experience that does not disappoint takers, and one which they will long remember. Dancie is packed and ready to take a cruise to Bermuda. She is confident that when she takes off for two weeks, she will have left Dancie's Place in good, capable hands.

***

Last month Miss Circe opened a bed and breakfast next door, complete with a canopy covered walkway leading to the side porch of her establishment. For visitors needing a place for an overnight stay and a satisfying meal, Miss Circe is there to serve them. She conceived the idea of a bed and breakfast after the construction boom brought so many new temporary residents to Hawk Town. Since the grand opening of this addition to her existing business, there has not been a night that the four bedrooms have stood empty. Some of the men who fell in love with the area return with their spouses or significant others to showcase the results of the construction that kept them away from home for so many months. Hawk Town, for them, has become a vacation spot of sorts because usually when they are visiting, a trip to nearby Bottomsail Beach is included in the adventure. And Miss Circe couldn't be happier with the success this new addition has brought to her business.

***

Joe Bailey had to choose between self-satisfaction and his daughter's happiness. As most fathers who have spoiled daughters do, Joe decided in favor of Patricia's happiness over his own. He feels that he has had a good life and most of his hopes and dreams have been fulfilled. His strongest desire at this stage in his life is to ensure Patricia has a satisfying life full of peace, happiness, and love. So, if Charlie is the man she has chosen to love, and whom she believes loves her in return, it's not Joe's place to interfere. He and Patricia have always maintained a mutual loving relationship, and Joe does not want that to be destroyed in his old age.

After the trial, and Charlie's vindication by the hand-picked jury, Patricia and Charlie were married in a quiet ceremony at the Bailey mansion. It was a warm, sunny day and the ceremony was held outdoors in the rose garden. Patricia radiated beauty and hope for a lifetime of happiness with Charlie. Charlie, of course, as usual, was the great charlatan. As he stood in the rose garden waiting to say, "I do," his thoughts were already forging months ahead of the present. Charlie was envisioning himself standing on the state capitol steps saying, "I do," as he is taking the oath of office.

The next election for the senate seat in the Teaville district is 18 months away. Everyone is left to wonder if Charlie's greatest dream will be fulfilled at that time. As for Patricia, she will be happy playing the role of Mrs. Charlie Pittman, whatever outcome is delivered by those election results.

During the months following their wedding and leading to the next election, Charlie and Patricia campaigned throughout the district in hopes of winning the senate seat. Many folks in the district have become skeptical of Charlie's honesty and worth after the death of his first wife, Natalie. They remember that Charlie had been charged with murdering his wife, even though he was not convicted. However, the fact that there had been enough evidence to bring charges against him left a cloud of suspicion hanging over Charlie's head in some folks' minds. It is doubtful that those who still believe Charlie is guilty, and those who remain unsure, will be voting for Charlie Pittman for the Xenolina Senate on Election Day.

***

John Riverbank and Eva Robinson dated for several years, during which time they fell in love. John proposed and Eva said, "Yes." They lived in John's house in Dillington for six months, and then the Goodrock home in Anderson was put on the market for sale. Both John and Eva love the country, and John couldn't believe this fantastic opportunity when it happened that he could purchase a stately home less than a mile from his parents' home. Without hesitation, John and Eva made an offer to the Realtor the first day the listing appeared on the market. Their offer was accepted, plans were made to move into the house as soon as they could complete some refurbishing and remodeling of the old-fashioned kitchen and bathrooms. And as soon as the work was completed, they moved into what is now their new forever home.

John and Eva agreed that they did not want to sell their home in Dillington, where they had lived through the first year of their marriage. They placed a for rent sign on the property once all of their belongings had been moved to Anderson. During this time there has been an exodus from northern cities as families have discovered Dillington near the beach, and don't want to leave the area once they have seen what it has to offer. It has been less than one month since the sign was placed in their yard in Dillington and the house has been rented to a young couple from New Hampshire.

John really likes the fact that even though Eva is principal of Granite Point Elementary School, she is down to earth and unpretentious. They are enjoying life in Kinder County, as both of their work schedules allow time for them to engage in some of their favorite pastimes together.

**

Zack Green retired two years ago and established a private detective agency. His agents work tirelessly because of certain cases involving moral turpitude that are commonplace in Kinder County. The majority of Zack's cases involve adulterous situations and subsequent divorce settlements. There aren't many southern rural counties that can outpace Kinder County when it comes to courting secretively with another person's spouse. The phrase "Love thy neighbor" seems to be misconstrued dramatically.

When his business is slow, and it rarely is, Zack volunteers at the Kinder County Sheriff's Department, mostly as a means of keeping in touch with old friends and keeping an eye on Casper, who works there as a student volunteer since he is planning to pursue a degree in criminal justice.

Last week when Shirley met Zack for lunch at the sheriff' department, she saw Casper for the first time in her life, and was taken aback over how much he resembles his father. She introduced herself to Casper and invited him to join them for lunch. She had prepared more than enough for two people. Zack chimed in to agree with Shirley, and Casper accepted her invitation. Lunch for the three of them that day was akin to a family reunion where one meets a new relative for the very first time.

***

Lizzie is spending her days in Silverboro in an institution for psychologically disturbed individuals. She lives in a world of fantasy and on any given day she imitates storybook characters. Today, she is Little Bo Peep and has been destroying property in search of what she believes she has lost. Two attendants have subdued her and placed her in a straightjacket until she can be calmed enough to move about less restrictively in her small cell.

Lizzie's psychotic episodes happen as frequently today as they have since the day Zack Green had her transported to Silverboro. It is doubtful that she will ever be released. Her prognosis continues to be one of gloom and doom.

***

Hugh is spending the final years of his life in a prison 500 miles from Kinder County. He rarely has a visitor, and he prefers it that way. Hugh spends most of his days idle. He dreams of what might have been if the rest of his life could have been spent wrapped in the arms of Agatha instead of being wrapped in four prison walls.

***

To this day, no one has seen or heard from Clemis Stapleton. There have been many prognosticators predicting Clemis' whereabouts or what might have happened to him. Some believe Clemis actually did go to New York and that he found a way to make moonshine and wine, which he is selling to bars as well as individuals. Others who feel that Clemis fled to New York believe Clemis was swallowed up by the big city and is now an unidentified statistic in an unmarked grave on Long Island.

Then there are those who don't believe Clemis ever made it to New York. They believe Clemis is somewhere in New Jersey or Philadelphia working as a farm laborer—he might even be a migrant farm worker, they say.

The old boys at Buster's Place from time to time, bounce around the idea that Clemis probably finally met a lonely, love-starved woman, a Sugar Mama, who has taken him in and is keeping him all to herself.

Peggy, who eventually overheard rumors that Clemis had murdered the two school teachers, has never believed that tale, and she often dreams about her daddy, but she never shares her dreams with anyone. By now she has given up hope of ever seeing him again, and every night when she says her prayers, she prays that wherever her daddy is, he is safe.

Whatever happened to Clemis Stapleton remains a mystery that most likely will never be solved.

In towns and neighborhoods in Kinder County, in the state of Xenolina, inhabitants harbor sins and secrets that disrupt and influence the daily lives of longtime residents, as well as those of newcomers, both rich or poor. Arson, murder, suicide, adultery, poisonings, honky tonks and houses of ill repute swirl around the present and future of established greedy family members and innocent households alike. Not all criminal cases will be solved--some may remain a mystery.

ABOUT THE AUTHOR

R. M. Shiver is a native of Rocky Point, North Carolina. Following her retirement from the position of Director of Social Services for Pender County in 2016, she published her first book, *Kinder County*, in 2017. Inspiration for that book's contents was based on facets of her true-life experiences and the antics of individuals she encountered along her life's journey. *Kinder County: Sins and Secrets,* while not a sequel to the first book, some of the tales are based upon stories she recalls from her childhood, blended with some events that happened later. Since retiring, her pastime has been writing, and this second book is equally as revealing as the first. She lives near the Northeast Cape Fear River in southeastern North Carolina with her 16-year-old grandson.